TeRRoR
in Branco Grande

zonder**kidz**.
The children's group of Zondervan

www.zonderkidz.com

Terror in Branco Grande
Copyright © 1996 by Jerry Jenkins

Requests for information should be addressed to:
Grand Rapids, Michigan 49530

Library of Congress Cataloging-in-Publication Data

Jenkins, Jerry B.

Terror in Branco Grande / Jerry B. Jenkins
      p. cm.— (AirQuest adventures; bk. 2)
     Summary: Kate senses trouble even before her father agrees to transport "relief sup-
plies" to South America, and when he is arrested, she and her brother attempt to prove
his innocence.
     ISBN-13: 978-0-310-71346-3 (softcover)
     ISBN-10: 0-310-71346-3 (softcover)
     [1. Smuggling—Fiction. 2. Brothers and sisters—Fiction. 3. Adventure and
adventurers—Fiction. 4. South America—Fiction. 5. Christian life—Fiction.] I. Title.
II. Series: Jenkins, Jerry B. AirQuest adventures ; bk. 2..
PZ7.J4138Te 2006
[Fic]--dc22

                                              2006005631

Art direction: Laura Maitner-Mason and Julie Chen
Illustrations: Dan Brown
Interior design: Ruth Bandstra

Printed in the United States of America

07 08 09 • 5 4 3 2

AirQuest **Adventures**

TERROR
in Branco Grande

Jerry B. Jenkins

zonder**kidz**

ZONDERVAN.COM/
AUTHOR**TRACKER**

To Sammy, Maya, and Elle, my hearts.

Contents

Women's Intuition

"You can't talk to me that way!" Kate Michaels said.

Her brother Chad sneered. "Just stop trying to act like Mom!"

Kate felt her face redden and a sob rise in her throat. She wanted to lash out, but she knew she would burst into tears. "What would be so wrong with acting like Mom?" she said. Just saying "Mom" brought back all the grief and pain of her mother's death six months before.

"Because you're not her! Nobody is or ever will be, so quit trying to be a woman or anything but a kid! And don't forget—you're not Thomas Edison, either!"

That was all Kate could take. She bounded up the steps to her room. As she flew by Dad at his desk, he said, "What are you two arguing about now?"

Kate slammed her door and flopped onto her bed. She allowed herself to cry softly, occasionally pausing to listen for Dad. Nothing. Maybe he was already giving Chad the standard lecture about girls and their emotions. Dad was real big on their sticking together as the AirQuest Adventures team. "We're family. We're all we've got," he always said.

Kate had just started sixth grade at Mukluk Middle School in northern Alaska. She felt older and more mature than ever; sometimes she almost forgot she was almost a year younger than Chad. So if she acted like her mom sometimes, what was wrong with that?

Her mom had been killed by a drunk driver one day when they were scheduled to pick up Dad at the airport. Dad, then an Air Force fighter pilot and owner of his own charter-flight company, was returning from a military assignment.

Since their mother's death, Kate's father had retired from military work and sold the company. Dad, Chad, and Kate had then formed AirQuest Adventures, a team available to Christian organizations anywhere in the world.

Dad was the pilot, of course. Chad, who his dad liked to call Spitfire after the quick and deadly World War II plane, was the computer expert. And Kate, a techie for as long as she could remember, knew a lot about radios and communications. She had won first prize at the school science fair every year since second grade.

Recently, she'd designed a two-way wrist radio that looked like a big watch. She and Chad and Dad all had one. After school Kate had told Chad that it wouldn't take much to add a miniature high frequency band and video camera to the gadget, which would allow for a crude LCD television picture.

Chad didn't believe her, which is what had started their argument a few moments before.

"Yeah, right." Chad had laughed as he followed her into the kitchen after school. "Like we could see each other on our wrist radios."

"Why is that so hard to believe?" she said. "We have cell phones where we can see each other—and even take pictures and make video clips."

"Exactly," Chad said. "So why waste time inventing a two- or three-way radio with a TV screen?"

"Think," Kate said, rolling her eyes. "Where we fly—jungles mostly—have you seen a lot of cell phone towers? Would your fancy phone be able to communicate at all?" She snorted. "You'd never pick up a signal."

Chad frowned. "True..."

Kate smiled. She loved proving him wrong. "Course, when we're talking into the radios, the other person could only see our mouth and nose, but if you held it back a ways, it would give a picture of our face or whole body."

Chad shook his head. "You're dreaming. The smallest two-way radio is ten times the size of your watch, and the smallest video camera is five times bigger than our wrist radios! How are you going to fit the machinery in there to record and send? And think of the antenna you'd need. We'd look like robots with rabbit ears!"

"You're not up on technology," Kate said. "They now make video cameras smaller than the end of your thumb. Batteries today will give you a five-mile range, and I know more than a hundred interference eliminator codes so we can hear each other clearly. Thanks to Dad, I also know the specs for military radios and what's needed to operate in harsh environments. I'm close, Chad, that's all I can say. You used to encourage me. Can't you see how it might work?"

"That's a long time away."

"No, it isn't! A Korean company has already invented a watch with a digital camera and phone. And video cameras in wristwatches already exist. I want to combine the watch and the video, but with a radio transmitter instead of a phone. The picture wouldn't be much, but it would be a start."

Chad shook his head. "It might make something interesting for this year's science fair, but you're years from making all that work."

"Maybe," Kate said. "I'm just saying I've got a feeling I'm on to something."

"You've got a feeling!" Chad spat. "You still think you've got women's intuition like Mom did?"

"Why shouldn't I? I'm a woman."

He laughed. "Not yet! Women's intuition is just a myth, and anyway"—and this is where he'd said it—"stop trying to act so much like Mom!"

Face down on her bed, Kate finally stopped crying. She sat up. The key was the battery! If she could somehow boost the power of those tiny batteries, she could transmit high-frequency radio waves plenty strong enough to produce an LCD readout.

As she started back down the stairs she saw that Dad was still at his desk. "What's up, Kate?" he said idly.

"I don't want to talk about it," she said.

Dad laughed, and she whirled to face him.

"Oh, come on, Katie. Don't give me that look. I just know that when you say you don't want to talk about something, it doesn't necessarily mean you don't want to talk about it."

Kate didn't know whether to smile or cry. Of course he was right. She shrugged. "I'll be in my workshop."

"And I'll be down in a few minutes to talk to you about whatever it is you want to talk to me about but say you don't. Fair enough?"

She rolled her eyes, then nodded and walked away. Men!

As she headed toward her frigid basement workshop, she heard Dad call out. "Spitfire! Got a minute?"

Downstairs, Kate lost herself in studying various combinations of batteries and experimenting with them to see what changes might show up on an oscillograph. She looked up when Chad came down.

"I don't know how you can stand it down here," he said, rubbing his arms.

"People think better in the cold," she said. "It's been proven."

"Yeah? So is your wrist TV done?"

"I'm probably a week away," she said.

"Yeah, well, I'm sorry for what I said about Mom and everything."

"What you said about *me*, you mean?"

"You know what I mean."

"Did Dad make you apologize?"

"What if he did?"

"Then don't bother."

Chad stared at the floor. "Well, I mean it anyway."

"Okay then. I accept. You don't need to hang around. Just go."

Chad appeared grateful and charged back up the stairs. A few minutes later, Dad showed up in her workshop. "So are you and Chad okay?"

"We're okay." Kate said, sighing. "We just get on each other's nerves."

"You figure you both miss Mom and need someone to take it out on?"

"Maybe."

"You can take it out on me," Dad said. "I can take it. That's what dads are for. You're supposed to give me grief."

"But Chad's easier to fight with and be mad at. He deserves it."

They both laughed. "Let's all try to do what Mom would want us to do, hmm?" Dad said. "That way it's like she's still with us."

Kate nodded and pursed her lips. "You always tell us to do what God wants us to do."

"What God wants us to do and what Mom would want us to do are pretty much the same, aren't they?"

"It always seemed that way," Kate said.

"It's even more true now. Listen," he said, "I need to talk to you about something else. I want to do a short weekend run to South America for that couple who wrote us last summer."

"Oh, Dad!"

"I know you've had a funny feeling about it, Kate, but there's no reason to worry."

"I thought you told them we were all still recuperating from the last trip."

"I did, but they've written again. They couldn't find anyone else to fly them and their relief supplies into that newly formed country down there. Don't worry. It sounds like something right up our alley. We don't even have to bring them back. They're planning to stay down there awhile."

That night after dinner, Dad read out loud the first letter he had received from Howard and June Geist. "'Our humanitarian organization, New Frontiers, Inc., head–quartered in Boise, Idaho, delivers goods to struggling Third World nations. We are looking for someone who can fly us and our goods into Branco Grande, capital city of the newly formed South American country of Amazonia. The country gets its name from the Amazon River.'"

Dad explained that Amazonia was way south, a land-locked country that appeared to have been cut out of the country of Argentina. It lay about midway between Buenos Aires, Argentina, and Santiago, Chile. The country had been formed after a fierce battle for independence from Argentina.

"I thought you already told them we wouldn't do it," Chad said.

"I did," Dad said. "They wrote back. Let me see here, 'We followed your advice and looked into other possibilities for getting into Amazonia with our supplies, but so far we have struck out.' They say the government of the new country is welcoming them with open arms because of the goods and supplies they're bringing." He laid his hands flat on the table. "I'm going to rent a six-seat Learjet and offer to fly them down there for free."

Kate frowned. "Didn't we have a policy about helping only Christian organizations?"

"Remember what Jesus said about feeding the hungry or visiting the prisoners?" Dad spoke quietly.

"You mean—like what we do for others is like doing it for Jesus?" Chad said.

"I know, I know," Kate mumbled. "But it just doesn't feel right ... "

"What?" Dad looked at her closely. "You still got a problem with this?"

"We just don't know these people," she said. "Why can't they find another way down there? How do they get to the other countries they go to?" Kate felt a rising panic. She couldn't bring herself to say it out loud, but she was also worried about getting into another airplane. How could Dad and Chad even think about flying after their crash only a few short months before in Indonesia?

"They sound legitimate to me," Dad went on. "It's a rough time of their year, they say. Donations are down, and people don't know enough about Amazonia to give money for relief work there. They're looking for a one-way ride down there for themselves and less than a thousand pounds of cargo."

"Well," Chad said, "I'm not interested in getting another bunch of shots."

Shots? That's just an excuse, Kate thought. Chad must be scared to fly too.

"I already checked on that," Dad said. "The shots we got for Indonesia cover all and more than we would need for South America."

"You already checked?" Kate said. "So we're going and that's it? Why don't you quit pretending it makes any difference what we think or say?"

Dad seemed to think about that. Chad looked amazed that Kate had spoken up like that to Dad.

"I care what you think, Kate," Dad said. "But if it really is just a feeling, what am I supposed to tell the Geists? 'My son and I are for it and willing even to provide the flight for free, but my daughter has a funny feeling about it, so no, we're sorry'?"

Was she just being a wimp? She knew Chad would never say anything even if he was afraid.

"Should I tell them we'll do it?" Dad said. "Either we all go, or we all stay home. That's been the deal since we formed the company. I won't leave you behind."

Kate was silent. Dad would probably take her silence as agreeing to go, but she could no longer fight for no real reason.

After homework and another hour in her workshop, Kate went to bed, and Dad came in to pray and talk as usual. "Don't feel bad about being cautious, Kate," he said. "Your mom was cautious. Or at least she was thorough. Everything was planned out and thought through. Remember that?"

Kate nodded, hoping Dad couldn't see the fear in her eyes in the low light.

"She always thought I was impulsive," Dad said. "It's okay to be cautious. The Bible calls it being prudent. But in this case I don't think you have any reason to be afraid."

"I'm—I'm—"

"What is it, Kate?" Dad said gently.

"I'm scared, Dad. The plane ... I mean ... your friend was killed, and we almost died."

Dad nodded. "Of course. It makes perfect sense that you'd be afraid."

"Aren't you and Chad? Even a little?"

"I'd be lying if I said no. But flying is all I've ever wanted to do. I can't let fear stop me from being who I am. Besides, we're a team. Does AirQuest Adventures go out of business at the first sign of trouble? When you fall off a horse—"

Kate could feel a lecture coming on. "When do we meet these people?" she said.

Dad smiled. "That's my girl. We meet them in Boise the last Friday of next month, and we take off for South America early the next morning. I'm chartering a small jet that will carry the five of us and their cargo."

Kate hadn't meant to imply she was all for it.

A week later Kate had a breakthrough on her wrist TV idea. When she finally was able to boost the power in the tiny batteries without damaging the other functions, she produced a crude image on a small liquid-crystal display. She yelled for Dad and Chad to come down to her workshop, and they were amazed.

"Will it work on a smaller display so you can fit it on our wrists?" Chad said.

"If I can get the parts I need in time, I'll have three of them made before we leave for South America."

Over the next few weeks she finished fashioning the wrist TVs.

When she finally met the Geists at their home in Boise, Idaho, her fears about them nearly vanished. Howard Geist was a big, burly man with white hair, a red face, and a constant smile. His wife was tall and thin, freckle-faced, and wore no makeup. Her eyes sparkled, especially when she talked to Chad or Kate.

Mrs. Geist showed Kate a scrapbook with snapshots of several deliveries she and her husband had made to various needy countries. Later the Geists showed Dad, Chad, and Kate sample packages of the seeds and medicines they planned to load onto the plane in the morning.

"Listen," June Geist said, "one thing we insist on. We're so grateful for your help that we want to bring meals along for the flight."

"Thanks," Dad said. "We appreciate it."

"The pleasure is all ours," June Geist said.

By the end of the evening, as the AirQuest Adventures team settled into their hotel room to wait for the next morning's flight, Kate's uneasiness was almost gone. Still, she had trouble falling asleep. Maybe she was just nervous about another flight into a mountainous country that would remind her of Indonesia. But like Dad said, "you can't let fear stop you."

Kate's nervousness was still there the next morning, but she tried to be cheerful. Nobody liked a grumpy person, especially at the start of a long flight. The Geists seemed upbeat as they pulled their rented truck into the hangar and began to load their cargo onto the plane.

Dad offered to help, but they insisted he finish filing his flight plan. Kate and Chad tried to help too, but the metal containers that fit so well together were too heavy. The kids piled into the small jet and sat in the back two seats. Kate's heart pounded so hard, she was sure Chad could hear it.

As Mr. Geist hoisted one of the containers in through the cargo door, he called out to Kate and Chad. "Would you mind if my wife and I sit back there? We want to be able to keep an eye on the cargo and the food."

Kate and Chad looked at each other and shrugged. "Sure," they said. Just then one of the cartons slipped out of Mr. Geist's grasp and bounced on the floor. The latches came loose and the top slid off, spilling out three small boxes. Howard Geist turned and hefted one end of another carton, and his wife grabbed the other end. He smiled at Kate and nodded at the boxes on the floor. "Would you mind picking those up for me, sweetie?" Kate bristled at being called *sweetie*, but she picked up the boxes anyway, which she noticed contained seed packets.

Soon everyone was on board. Kate and Chad, now in the middle seats, passed their backpacks to the rear to be stowed with Dad's. The Geists tucked everything in the cargo pile along with their own bags.

Dad checked to make sure the cargo was secure, then started the engines. Kate turned to Chad. "Are you scared? You know, of flying?"

He just stared straight ahead, but his hands were gripping the armrests, and his knuckles were white.

Branco Grande

The Geists sat in the back for the entire flight, while Kate and Chad moved between the middle two seats and the seat next to Dad. Once they were in the air for a while, Kate's tension began to ease. She got to know the Geists better, chatting with them off and on for hours. When the couple wanted to nap, she talked with Chad or just sat next to Dad and pretended to be his first officer.

"Where are we staying, Dad?"

He handed her a brochure from his flight bag. "The Branco Grande Plaza del Rio, a new standard of hospitality in a new country," she read. Inside was a photo of a beautiful hotel under construction in the capital city. One wing was finished, and the brochure showed a pool and a little park beside it. Three other wings were framed up, and an artist had drawn pictures of what they would look like when they were finished.

"Really?" Kate said. "We're staying here?"

Dad nodded and smiled. "We roughed it in Indonesia. I wanted this trip to be fun for you kids."

"Thanks, Dad."

Kate put on her headphones and listened to the radio air traffic as they flew over the larger cities in North America, Central America, and South America. She was grateful that the international language of aviation was English.

Now that she wasn't as nervous, Kate even grew drowsy and fell asleep with the headphones on, occasionally rousing when static or voices came through. When Dad reached over and slid the earphones off her head, she curled up and slept soundly, making up for the restless night before.

Kate didn't know how long she had slept when the landing woke her. Though the jet was air conditioned, heat invaded the cabin. Kate peered out, squinting against the late afternoon sun that made heat waves shimmer off the end of the runway. She peeled off her sweater and found she was already sweating heavily. It seemed strange to see only a few other planes at the Branco Grande airstrip.

"That huge, long runway," her dad said, pointing, "was built for the jumbo jets the new government hopes to begin flying to their new capital city soon."

In the distance Kate saw the airport: a row of low buildings, some finished, some not. The airport personnel wore camouflage uniforms. Kate watched as they unloaded a cargo plane near a crude metal shed. Several open-topped, four-wheel drive jeeps waited nearby. Four men carrying automatic assault weapons were in each jeep. "Dad?" she said, voice quivering.

But Dad had one hand up to his headphones. "Roger, understand," he was saying. "Roger, understand."

Kate grabbed her earphones and listened. Someone was telling Dad in broken English to stay right where he was, to not taxi toward the airport. "We will come and inspect your plane on the runway," the voice told Dad.

"Roger that, understand," Dad said. One of the four-manned vehicles roared out from under a rough shelter of leaves and branches and into the sunshine. The driver swerved recklessly while the other three men desperately held on. Kate heard the jeep's squealing brakes from inside the still-pressurized cabin. The vehicle finally stopped directly in front of the jet.

The jeep's three passengers cautiously stepped out and brandished their weapons while the driver reached for a bullhorn. "Are you carrying any weapons?"

Dad shook his head and raised his hands.

"The others?" the driver demanded.

Kate and Chad and the Geists all followed Dad's example and raised their hands.

"I'm going to talk to ground control and get to the bottom of this." Dad reached for the microphone, but the gunman to their left rattled three loud bursts from his weapon into the air.

Dad quickly raised both hands again, and the driver shouted through his bullhorn. "Don't do that again!" he said. "You want to get yourself and your passengers killed? We could blow you off the runway with one grenade!"

Dad had to know they couldn't hear him, Kate thought, but he shouted back, "There are children on this plane, and we're on a humanitarian mission. We demand appropriate respect and hospitality!"

"Silence!" The driver reached beneath his seat and displayed a grenade. "We know who you are, and we are merely taking normal precautions! We will check your plane and your cargo, and then we will process your passengers in customs."

"Customs," Dad muttered. "I can't wait to see that facility."

"I ask again—do you or any of your passengers have weapons?"

Dad shook his head.

"If we find any, you could be sentenced to death!"

"Chad, did you bring your AK–47?" Dad whispered.

"Not this time, Dad," Chad said. "Seemed like a little too much power."

"Depressurize, and then keep your hands in the air while we do our work!"

The driver stayed in the jeep, and a gunman stood at each wing while the third yanked open the cargo door. "Do not be afraid, everybody," he said, as he dug through the cargo. The muscular young man was dark with long hair and a scraggly black beard. Sweat had soaked through his shirt. "Please face the front, señorita," he said, glancing at Kate. "No problem. No problem." He loosened the latches on the big metal containers and slid off the tops. "Seeds, more seeds, seeds, medicine, more seeds," he said over and over. "*Bueno, bueno, gracias.* Sandwiches! May I?"

"Like we've got a choice!" Dad mumbled.

Mrs. Geist insisted that the man help himself and share the goodies with his friends. He tossed food to his compatriots, then began to search backpacks and suitcases, tossing them on the ground as he finished each one. He ignored the larger cargo containers in the plane.

Dad rapped on the window. "Hey, take it easy with our bags!" he shouted.

The driver tossed the grenade onto the jeep seat and, still holding the bullhorn, he picked up his weapon. He stepped from the jeep and walked directly to the cockpit, where he pressed the barrel against the window. Kate covered her face with her hands and shrank down in the seat.

"Sit up, señorita!" the man shouted, and she did.

"The window is bulletproof," Dad whispered, "and he knows that."

"And you," the man said to Dad. "Unless you keep your hands in the air, I will kill you. Comprendé?"

Dad nodded but stared at the man in disgust. "Why terrorize my passengers? They're civilians and kids!"

"Are you calling me a terrorist?" the man shouted.

"You're terrorizing them."

"No more talking! Paco! You finished?"

The young man in the cargo hold said he was, but then whistled and marched dramatically around to the front of the plane. He held a semi-automatic pistol by the barrel in two fingers. "Look what I find in this bag!" he crowed.

The backpack was Dad's, but the gun was not. "Whose is that?" Dad said, almost under his breath.

Howard Geist's face was redder than ever. "Surely you didn't bring that."

"Of course not. It's a plant."

The man with the bullhorn waved Paco over and peered at the weapon in the sunlight. "American-made Smith & Wesson," he said. "And found in the bag of... " He turned the identification tag over and read slowly, "Bruce Michaels of Mukluk, Alaska. Which one of you is that?"

Dad nodded and gestured to himself. "But that is not my gun. I don't own a Smith & Wesson, and I did not carry a weapon on this plane."

"You may explain it in customs," the soldier said.

"I can't," Dad said. "Someone planted it."

"You would accuse us of such a thing?" yelled the man with the bullhorn. "You bring a powerful firearm into my country, and you accuse me of that? Paco! Drag him out of there!"

Dad dropped his hands and dug in his flight bag until he found his wallet. He pulled out their passports and visas, then slipped the wallet to Kate. "Wrap this in your sweater," he said, "and whatever you do, keep it hidden."

"Hands up!" Bullhorn shouted from the ground. Kate tucked the heavy wallet into the back of her sweater and rolled the sweater up, tying it around her waist. She and Dad raised their hands again as Paco opened the cockpit door on Kate's side. "Move back, little lady," he said.

She unbuckled her seat belt and stepped between the seats to sit next to Chad. As she moved, she felt the wallet pulling on the rolled up sweater around her waist. Would Paco see it? She was afraid it would flop out, and she quickly dropped into the seat.

"You!" Paco shouted at Dad. "Out! Out!"

Paco grabbed Dad's wrist and pulled him over the seat. Dad stumbled out of the plane.

"Hands up! Search!"

Dad raised his hands yet again, and Paco patted him down. "Any more guns in the plane?"

Dad shrugged. "The only one I've seen is the one your people put there."

Paco pressed his weapon against Dad's neck, and Kate froze. "I could kill you where you stand."

"But you have no reason to. You must have planted the gun for some kind of leverage." Dad glanced over his shoulder. "Now that you've got it, what do you want? Or are you just a soldier and not a commander?

"You'll be just as dead no matter which I am. Now move!"

As the men handcuffed Dad and pushed him toward the jeep, Kate heard Bullhorn call on his radio for another vehicle and more help to unload the cargo. Within a minute, more soldiers arrived. The Geists and Chad were herded into one jeep, and Kate was put into the back seat of another— she sat directly behind the driver, the man with the bullhorn. Dad sat in the front next to Bullhorn, and Paco climbed in beside Kate. *Dear God, help us!* She could hardly move; their luggage was stashed all around them. Every chance she got, Kate tightened the sweater around her.

Kate watched the unloading operation, and then the same thing happened that had happened in the hangar in

Boise. One of the containers popped open, and some boxes fell out. The weight shifted, and the two men lugging the container almost dropped it.

"Paco!" Bullhorn said. "Help them."

Paco jumped from the vehicle, and Kate realized no one was watching her. She worked the wallet out of her sweater and stuffed it down between the seat cushion and the back of the seat. Then she pressed her back against it until it was completely buried in the cushion. She hooked her toe into her own backpack and slowly slid it in between her feet. She had packed all three wrist TVs, and she didn't want them found. Kate pushed on the backpack until it was lodged out of sight behind the seat.

"I don't want to be separated from my kids," Dad said. "That's my son in the other jeep."

"We don't care what you want, señor. You have been found trying to smuggle a weapon into our country. Bringing in a weapon is not in itself against our new constitution. Many mercenaries and freedom fighters have come in to help us defend ourselves. But you must declare it."

Dad just shook his head.

"We are not unreasonable people," Bullhorn said. "We will determine why you wanted to smuggle a weapon in, which side you are sympathetic with, and whether you should be sentenced to death or just life in prison."

Kate couldn't believe this! But Dad turned quickly and shook his head at her, as if to say that was ridiculous—the man was bluffing.

"Oh, you think I am not serious, señor? Wait till you see your cellmates. May I assume you sympathize with Argentina?"

"I know nothing about your revolution. From the news and the fact that the United States government is considering recognizing your sovereignty, I can only assume your cause was just."

"That is the correct answer, señor. But gun smuggling does not fit. You had better hope we find no more contraband in your cargo."

Kate could only guess what *sovereignty* and *contraband* meant. The other vehicle had already pulled away with the Geists and Chad aboard. She knew Dad was as anxious as she was to be reunited with Chad.

And what a mess for the poor Geists. Here they were, trying to do something nice for the people of a new country, and they were treated like criminals.

Despite her fear, Kate felt suddenly tired. She only wished she could go back to her nap and discover that this was all a dream. A bad dream.

The Tribunal

Kate's heart raced as she thought about her dad's wallet stuffed into the seat behind her and her backpack hidden deep under the seat. It had scared her to see Chad squatting between Howard and June Geist, who sat in the two back seats of the other four-wheel drive, which was crammed with armed guards and roaring off toward the terminal.

Something felt strange about the way the Geists had seemed to relax in their seats. She was trying to make sense of it when Dad turned to the man with the bullhorn. "I do not want to be separated from my son," he said fiercely.

Bullhorn started the jeep. "Señor, you have no say in—"

Dad jerked sideways. "Okay, fine! I'll walk. I will not be separated!" He swung his legs over the side of the vehicle and staggered onto the runway. But after two quick steps toward the terminal a quarter mile away, he stopped in his tracks at the sound of gunfire behind him.

"Dad!" Kate screamed and covered her ears. It was Bullhorn who had fired into the air. He jumped from the jeep.

"If you are dead," he shouted, "you will be separated from both of your children forever!"

Dad whirled to face him. "I don't know what you people are trying to pull, but we have rights under international law!"

"You may have rights, but I have the weapon." He grabbed Dad by the handcuffs and swung him around, causing him to topple back into the vehicle. "You, your son, your daughter, and your other passengers will be inter– rogated together, so just calm down."

"Well, get moving then!" Dad said.

Paco had been leaning across Kate all this time, trying to see the action. He smiled broadly now and leaned back against the seat. Kate glared at him, fighting tears. Dad owned handguns—she had seen them. The huge Smith & Wesson was not one of them. She'd prove it was planted if it was the last thing she did.

Kate had seen a new side of her father, and it almost made her bold enough to speak up. But she was not as convinced as Dad seemed to be that these people would not shoot them. Two soldiers had already fired into the air, and she had seen and heard the spent cartridges plink onto the asphalt of the runway.

As the vehicle whipped around and sped toward the terminal, Kate grabbed the back of the seat in front of her to keep her balance. The last thing she wanted was to lean over onto Paco.

Kate's hands were inches from the driver's neck and the weapon strapped over his shoulder. But when she turned to steal a glance at Paco, he chuckled, as if reading her mind. How long could an eleven-year-old live if she attacked an armed soldier? All Kate could do was pray that everything would be straightened out in customs.

When the jeep jerked to a stop in front of the single-story terminal, Chad and the Geists were already being herded inside. Dad turned and gestured with a nod that Kate should stay close to him. *As if I would do anything else.*

Bullhorn and Paco jumped out first and stood on either side of the jeep, weapons in hand. Dad awkwardly stumbled from his seat to the ground, unable to steady himself with his hands cuffed behind his back. Bullhorn gestured to Kate, indicating that she should climb down out of his side of the vehicle, but she ignored him and scrambled into the front and out the same way Dad had gone. She stole a glance back at the jeep and saw a gap between the back and the cushion of her seat. But the wallet wasn't showing. She'd get it when they were driven back to the plane.

Kate realized that none of the vehicles had numbers or license plates and were all the same size and color. If they moved it, she wouldn't know that jeep from any of the others. She trotted to catch up with Dad as he hurried into the terminal, where he turned his head in every direction, obviously looking for Chad.

Bullhorn ordered Paco and a couple of other soldiers to bring in the luggage, and Kate found herself praying again. She could only hope the soldiers wouldn't think to look deep under the seat where they would find her backpack.

When Paco and Bullhorn steered Dad down a long hallway to a large room under a sign that read *Interrogación*, Kate peeked back to study the jeep. The left headlight was broken, and the bumper was creased. She hoped that wasn't true of any of the other jeeps. Soldiers began filing in with their luggage, and she saw no one with her backpack. She turned back around just in time to keep from bumping into Paco, who had stopped before the interrogation room.

Kate heard footsteps and turned to see three men and two women approaching from the other end of the hallway. They wore uniforms, and they all looked neater and less haggard than the soldiers. They filed into the room before anyone else and began setting up a tape recorder and their notebooks at one end of the table.

"Must I sit in there handcuffed in front of my children?" Dad said.

"Silence!" Bullhorn said. "You are now in the custody of General Rafael Valdez, and he will tell you whether you will remain cuffed or not."

General Valdez was a short, powerfully built man who stood quietly to one side as his aides finished arranging everything. He scowled at Dad, then asked Bullhorn a question in Spanish. Kate guessed he had asked why Dad was handcuffed, because Bullhorn was obviously rehashing what had happened on the runway. With a gesture and a nod, the general gave instructions to remove Dad's handcuffs. Paco did so and then stood with his weapon in both hands, as if afraid Dad would try something.

The older of the two women, who looked older than anyone in the room except perhaps the Geists, finally got the tape recorder plugged in. The general sat in the middle of one side of the table, flanked by a man on either side. The women sat at each end. Kate could hardly take her eyes off the younger woman. She strained to read the nameplate above her chest pocket—Eva Flores. Kate couldn't be sure, but she thought she saw a hint of sympathy or encouragement in the young woman's eyes. The rest of the people in uniform were grim-faced and quiet.

"Passports and visas, *por favor*," the older woman sang out.

The Geists produced theirs, and Dad turned over three sets. The woman flipped to the picture in each passport, glanced at the person, and pointed to a chair before the tribunal of officers. June Geist was placed at the far left end of five chairs. Then Howard Geist sat beside her. Dad was in the middle. Then Chad. Then Kate.

That put Kate directly in front of Eva Flores. More than once they caught each other's eyes, and Kate felt strangely warmed. Could she have found a caring person in the middle of this nightmare?

The older woman placed the passports before the general in the order in which the Americans sat. Valdez repeated the routine, peeking at each picture and matching it with the person before him. He glanced at the visas as well, then crossed his arms and sat staring at Dad. Dad did not look away.

Valdez nodded to the older woman, who turned on the tape recorder. In a thick accent, he began, "This is an official investigation by the government of the sovereign South American state of Amazonia into the possible illegal transport of weapons and contraband goods into the airport of the capital city of Branco Grande."

The general read off the number of Dad's rented Learjet and then read into the record the names of the passengers, starting with Kate.

"Kathryn Thompson Michaels, age eleven, a native of Enid, Oklahoma, currently residing in Mukluk, Alaska.

"Chadwick Whiteford Michaels, age twelve, a native of Enid, Oklahoma, currently residing in Mukluk, Alaska.

"Bruce Phillip Michaels, age thirty-five, a native of Kalamazoo, Michigan, currently residing in Mukluk, Alaska."

"Recently retired United States Air Force colonel," Dad added.

"Pardon?" Valdez said. "You, señor?"

"That is correct, sir."

"Then you should know it is a violation of international law to smuggle weapons or—"

"Of course I know that, sir. That's why I wouldn't do such a foolish thing. That weapon was planted—"

"Señor, this trial is only beginning. You will have your chance to—"

"Excuse me?" Dad leaned forward. "So this is a trial now?"

"What did you think it was?"

Kate's breath came in short gasps.

"Surely this must violate your own constitution! I haven't been formally charged, and I don't have a lawyer."

"Our constitution, señor, is still in process. Meanwhile, we are a nation not unlike your own, brought into existence with bloodshed at the hands of our oppressive, tyrannical enemy." He smiled grimly. "You sacrificed a lawyer when you lied about not having a weapon with you. All you had to do was declare it and swear allegiance to our cause. We would not even have required you to surrender it."

"You can have it," Dad said quietly, "because it's not mine."

One of the soldiers who had been rifling through the luggage hurried over and whispered in the general's ear. Valdez shot him a double take and whirled in his chair to talk animatedly with him. When he turned back, his face was flushed and his eyes afire.

"You, señor, will have an opportunity to speak later. Not only have more weapons been found among your luggage, but also cocaine and heroin. My patience with you is at an end."

"Your patience with *me*?" Dad shook his head. "But of course you knew about the drugs before they were found, right?"

"What a bunch of lies!" Chad shouted. "My dad would never do anything like—"

"Señor!" General Valdez shouted. "You will quiet your son, or you will be separated. Any further outbursts will be cause for an immediate judgment against you."

Dad put a hand on Chad's shoulder. "Son, let's just ride this out," he said quietly. "Something's happening here that's out of our control."

Eva Flores squinted, staring at Dad and Chad as if trying to make it all compute. Kate hoped the woman could see through all of this. But even if she had doubts, what could she do? Did she have any authority, or was she just an assistant to the general?

General Valdez picked up the fourth passport and flipped to the picture. "George Kennicott, age fifty-six, a native of Albuquerque, New Mexico, currently residing in Anchorage, Alaska."

George Kennicott? Kate turned to see her father's reaction. Who in the world was George Kennicott? Dad and Chad were staring at Howard Geist, or at least the man they thought was Howard Geist. He ignored them, holding the general's gaze and nodding slightly.

Dad let out a huge sigh and nodded slowly, as if it had all become clear to him. But it wasn't clear to Kate. What had Dad figured out? Were guns and drugs really found in the cargo, and had the Geists — or the Kennicotts — put them there?

The general continued. "Iris Kennicott, age fifty-five, a native of Baton Rouge, Louisiana, currently residing in Anchorage, Alaska."

So the Geists were using fake names, either with AirQuest Adventures or with the passport officials. Here Dad was accusing the Amazonians of framing him, and maybe it was really the Geists — or the Kennicotts — all along. Kate wanted to scream. Dad seemed to just take it all in.

The general turned to take a list from one of the soldiers. He studied it for a minute, then set it in front of him on the table. "Let's start with you, señora," Valdez said, addressing Mrs. Geist. "Mrs. Kennicott, your luggage contains no contraband and your papers are in order. Tell me the nature of your business in Amazonia."

"My husband and I run a humanitarian organization out of Anchorage called New Frontiers. We donate our time, along with medicine and seeds, to emerging countries. We are on file with your foreign ministry, and we were expected."

"How is it that you have traveled with a smuggler of weapons and drugs?"

"We had no idea. We advertised for a flight to Amazonia, and Mr. Michaels here answered the ad. He offered to fly us for free, and we couldn't pass up the bargain."

"That's not true!" Chad blurted, but Dad quieted him. The general continued. "Did you not suspect that someone offering to fly you for free might be using you as a cover for his own smuggling operation?"

"We never even gave that a thought. We had heard that Mr. Michaels was very successful with his business, the Yukon Do It air charter service, and we were grateful that he seemed interested in our humanitarian efforts."

Kate could tell from Chad's body language that he was not going to keep quiet about this. "That's a lie!" he shouted. "They live in Boise and they call themselves the Geists and my dad doesn't even have that business anymore. We call ourselves—"

"Enough!" Valdez shouted. "You will each get your turn."

Dad put a hand on Chad's shoulder and nodded.

"Mr. Kennicott?" the General said.

"Yes, Mr. Michael's manifest will show that he flew a small plane out of Mukluk, where he lives, to Anchorage, where he picked us up and rented the Lear."

"I didn't pick you up until we got to Boise, and you know it," Dad said.

"Anyway," the older man said, "it will also show that we made a stop in Boise, Idaho, which is where we warehouse our goods. As my wife has said, we had no idea that he and his children would be involved in anything but a straight charter flying service. If our papers are in order and our cargo is accounted for, we would ask that we be excused to go about our business."

Kate glared at the older couple. Why were they trusted while her family was treated like criminals? Surely the general would not let these people trick him like this. But he quickly slid their passports and visas down the table to Eva Flores, who began stamping them. The general stood and extended his hand to the couple Kate had known as the Geists.

"Mr. and Mrs. Kennicott, allow me to apologize for having detained you, but you understand."

The "Geists" stood and shook his hand.

"We understand," Mr. Kennicott said.

"And also allow me to welcome you to Branco Grande on behalf of the free and independent people of Amazonia and to thank you for the gifts you have brought us."

The Kennicotts made a big deal of nodding and looking humble as they smiled and picked up their documents, then hurried out.

Kate slumped, puzzled by her dad's sudden silence. If the Geists were the criminals, the real smugglers, and they were free, Kate wondered what that meant for her and her brother and her dad. She knew Dad had brought their original letter, with the name Geist on it, and she thought he had attached a newspaper article with a picture of them posing with some foreign dignitary. That also identified them as the Geists. Would the general change his mind if he saw that? And did she dare suggest that it was in Dad's wallet, stuffed in the seat of one of their own jeeps?

No, Dad had made it clear that she should keep his wallet hidden no matter what. He could always ask her for the wallet if he wanted to produce his proof. What was going to happen to her family? Dad would get his turn to talk, but what could he say? If he tried to blame this on the Geists, or whoever they were, he would get nowhere. The people who now called themselves the Kennicotts were already heroes to the Amazonians.

Kate sat on her hands, rocking on the hard wooden chair, sweating in the oppressive heat. She glanced at Eva Flores, whose forehead seemed knotted as she stared at the three passports still laid out in front of the general.

Kate tried to catch her eye, to find that hint of sympathy or encouragement, but Eva Flores was not looking at her.

The "Hearing"

Kate could hardly believe what had happened since they'd landed. Even if they didn't know who planted the guns and the drugs in their cargo, even if it was done after they landed, they did know the Geists were certainly not who they claimed to be. At the very least they were liars and impostors.

Kate watched Dad as he sat at the table shaking his head, while the general and his aides conferred. But Eva Flores merely listened and observed the others. A soldier approached and turned in yet another list of some kind, then whispered something to Valdez. The general nodded and gestured, and soon several soldiers filed in, pushing dollies containing the metal cargo containers the Geists had loaded onto the plane.

"This will prove we're innocent," Kate whispered to Chad. "Those containers aren't even ours!"

The general looked up quickly and scowled at her, and Eva Flores casually put a finger to her lips, as if to warn Kate to be quiet and careful. Whenever Eva Flores seemed to communicate in some way Kate felt secure; something about this woman made Kate want to trust her.

When the nearly one thousand pounds of metal containers were stacked in a corner, General Valdez turned to the soldiers. "Show me," he said.

Two soldiers set aside the loose tops and began pulling stuff from the containers. At first all they produced were boxes of seed packets, cartons of penicillin, and two kinds of medicines for what the Geists had said was the treatment of malaria. But then one soldier bent and, leaning his torso deep into one of the other containers, pulled out a wooden rack which held four high-powered assault weapons. The other soldier pulled boxes of ammunition from another container.

Kate peeked at her dad. He just sat there as if nothing would surprise him now.

"If you were bringing these into our country to aid us in the defense of our coup," General Rafael Valdez said, "you would be a hero to us. But as you have denied bringing them, it is too late to take credit. If it makes you feel any better, they will be put to good use."

"They are not mine," Dad said.

"Oh? And how do I know that? These are American-made weapons. A man of your stature in the military would have ready access to these."

"I'm no longer in the military, and anyone in the United States has access to such weapons. The right to bear arms is in—"

"Your constitution, yes, I know. Ours, too. So, if these are not yours, what is your explanation? And never let it be said that I did not give you an opportunity to stage your defense."

"This is my defense? I face so-called evidence I have never seen and must explain why it is not mine?"

"You had better say something, Señor Michaels. Your hours of freedom are fast closing."

Dad sighed and spoke in a flat, even tone. "I don't know who put weapons in those containers. I never saw them before they were loaded onto my plane. My son is correct in that the Kennicotts, as you call them, represented themselves to us as the Geists from Boise. We spent last evening in their home before leaving this morning. If their phony name and location is part of this, then yes, maybe those weapons were in the cargo from the time we left the States."

"You did not supervise the loading of cargo on your own plane?"

"I was doing the preflight checklist while they loaded the cargo—at their request, I might add—and they seemed to have a lot of experience at this sort of thing. I can see why now."

"Don't be pointing the finger at the Kennicotts, Señor Michaels. They are on register with our foreign ministry, and they come with the full authority of the President of the United States."

"What does that mean?"

"Here, look. But do not touch."

The general spun a single sheet of paper and slid it to where Dad could lean forward and read it. "A personal letter of introduction and endorsement from your president himself," the general said proudly.

"All due respect, General," Dad said, "but this is such an obvious phony that even you should be able to see through it."

It was clear the general was offended. He snatched up the sheet and ran his fingers along the embossed letterhead. Then he licked a finger and ran it across the signature. "See, the ink runs! It is an original. What is not to trust about it?"

"For one thing, the president of the United States is so isolated, so hard to get to, that it is highly unlikely any private citizen could get such an endorsement from him. Only an ambassador or an official spokesperson from our government would ever rate something like this. I'm sorry.

It's as phony as the Geists, or the Kennicotts, or whatever you choose to call them. If I'm guilty of a crime, it's that I have allowed myself to be royally duped."

"Señor," Valdez said, "you are guilty of much more than that." He wheeled around in his chair to watch as the soldiers began lifting cellophane bags from the containers. "In the Kennicotts' containers, medicines and seeds," Valdez said. "In your containers, cocaine and heroin, as well as weapons and ammunition."

"All those containers belong to the Geists'," Dad said. "My record is crystal clear from childhood. Other than two speeding tickets when I was a teenager, you'll find nothing there for thirty-five years. But I'll bet the Geists' record is not so clear."

"The Kennicotts are not your concern," Valdez said. "Your life had better be your concern. Our country has been in existence for less than a year, and we have executed more than two dozen smugglers of drugs and firearms."

Suddenly everyone grew quiet. Kate glanced at Chad, who looked pale.

Valdez stroked his mustache. "We have a slogan here that we picked up from our neighbors to the north, the Mexicans, and from your own country. It is called zero-tolerance. We do not tolerate threats to our freedom or to our health. Weapons that are not brought in here to help us hold off the tyrannists are here to bring us down. And drugs are brought here for only two reasons—to make the smuggler rich and to weaken the moral fabric of our society."

Suddenly, Dad leaned across the table, arms outstretched. "Listen to me, please," he said. "I agree with this policy a hundred percent. I've seen my own country go from being tough on crime to soft on crime. I know the Mexicans sentence international criminals to life in prison or to death, and they make it stick. But with just a little detective work you can prove or disprove my story."

Dad looked earnestly at the other officials, one at a time, then turned back to the general.

"You just let the real criminals walk free because you were duped like I was. I don't mean to offend or insult you, sir, but if you are sincere about the health of your country, you don't want to pin this crime on an innocent man. The smallest amount of detective work can tell you where those metal containers came from. You could fingerprint the contents. You could check out the, uh, the Kennicotts with the United States government."

"You forget that your government is still dragging its feet in recognizing us as a sovereign state."

"It's just a matter of time."

"We have allocated land for a U.S. embassy, but they have thumbed their noses at us."

"No! I'm certain I've read that it's just red tape, and that they will be appointing an ambassador soon."

"Let me ask you something, Señor Michaels. Do you think you are talking to an imbecile?"

Dad shook his head.

"Do you think you are talking to someone who does not hold your life in his hands?"

"I'm starting to get the picture."

"Are you?"

"Yes, sir."

"Do you understand that I have sentenced men both to life in prison and to death? And that it has been done right here in this room?"

Kate couldn't move, and it felt as if the air had been sucked from the room.

"No trial?" Dad said. "No jury? No lawyer for the accused?"

"Now you really are getting the picture. You do not talk to me with respect even though my men carry weapons. You do not talk to me with respect even though I hold the rank of general in my country's military. You do not talk to me with respect even when you have been caught red-handed, smuggling into my country. Maybe now you will talk to me with respect when you know I hold your life in my hands."

Kate wished with all her might that her dad would try to convince the general that it wasn't a lack of respect but rather the phony charges that were causing such strong reactions. But she knew Dad was not the type to back down from someone who was unfair and unjust.

"Of course I don't want to say or do anything that would cost my children their only remaining parent," Dad said, and Kate heard Eva Flores groan softly. She glanced up at the woman and saw the worried look in her eyes.

"These children have no mother?" General Valdez said.

"No, sir, she was killed in an auto accident earlier this year."

At this, Eva Flores quickly covered her mouth with her hand.

"All the more reason for you to come clean now, Señor Michaels," Valdez said. "If you refuse to take responsibility for your crimes, you will be sentenced to prison either for life or to await your execution, and your children will become wards of the state."

"He didn't do anything wrong!" Kate shouted, but her dad shushed her.

"General Valdez, if you imprison me or put me to death and detain my children, you will have the United States government and the court of world opinion against you. I am a decorated military officer with an impeccable record, a recent widower with two young children. And I

am innocent. Even if I were guilty, my government would
not allow one of its citizens, especially a retired Air Force
colonel, to be tried by a one-man judge and jury."

"You think I care about the court of world opinion? You
think I feel threatened by the United States? Had I been
in the battle over the Islas Malvinas years ago, they would
belong to Argentina now."

Dad looked puzzled. "You mean the Falkland Islands?"

"That may be what *you* call them, but—"

"That was a United Kingdom possession anyway, and—"

"But the U.S. aided them."

"It was long before my time," Dad said.

"As I suspected, you deny everything. Nothing is your
fault."

"Well, in the case of this cargo it certainly isn't."

"Señor," General Valdez said slowly, "you have spoken to
me with great indignation, as a man who has been wrongly
accused."

For the first time, Kate felt hope. The general's voice
sounded softer. Was he about to say that Dad could possibly
be telling the truth? That was what she read in the eyes of
Eva Flores, but were women the only ones with intuition?
The Bible said nothing about women's intuition, but Kate
knew her mother had had it, and Mom had always said she
believed it was a gift from God.

The general continued. "And though I would not willingly forge ahead with charges and sentencing of a man of your stature and face the reaction from your government and possibly the rest of the world, I am a man who has long fought in the face of tremendous odds. I might be tempted to be more sympathetic to what you say if your name were not fastened to every cargo container that carried guns or drugs."

"That's impossible."

The general waved over a soldier who had pulled identification tags from the containers.

The general read out loud, "Bruce Michaels, President, Yukon Do It Air Charter Service, Mukluk, Alaska. How do you explain these?"

"Not mine," Dad said.

The general laughed and pushed the pile of tags toward Dad.

Dad picked one up. "You ask me to speak to you with respect because of your rank, your weapon, your authority. But let me ask you a question you cannot answer."

"Go ahead. This is your day in court."

"Put yourself in my position. Let's say I'm guilty. I'm flying guns and drugs into this country using an air charter service and a humanitarian organization as my cover. Are you with me?"

"Don't insult me. Go on and ask your question."

"Okay, you are me. Would you put your name in with the contraband?"

The general stared, not smiling.

"I told you it was an unanswerable question," Dad said. "Of course you wouldn't. It would be stupid. And you are not stupid, are you, General? You're not stupid enough to go through with this."

Valdez sat seething. "Your children will live better than you will," he said, "at least for the brief time you are still alive."

"You're sentencing me to death? Because it appears I put my name and the name of a company I haven't owned for months on containers of smuggled goods?"

"I want you to think about your children living in one of our fine orphanages. And I want you to explain this." He turned again with a flourish and waved over another soldier who carried three backpacks. One was Dad's. One was Chad's. And the other Kate guessed had belonged to the Geists.

"Look here," Valdez said. "I would bet this is pure heroin." He lifted a huge plastic bag full of white powder from Dad's backpack. Then he looked at the identification tag on the backpack. It read, "Bruce Michaels, President, AirQuest Adventures, Mukluk, Alaska."

"That should be proof enough that this stuff was planted," Dad said. "Why would I use two different identification tags?"

Valdez shrugged and smiled. "The containers are older. You never switched the tags."

He pulled a similar plastic bag out of Chad's backpack. He read the tag. "Chad Michaels."

"That's not—" Chad began, but Dad quickly stopped him with a hand on his knee.

Valdez then pulled a bag from the Geists' backpack and turned the tag over. "Katie Michaels," he read, and Kate nearly jumped from her seat. Only her dad called her Katie, and they would never put that on an ID tag. Anyway, that wasn't her backpack.

"What else is in there?" Dad said, and Valdez turned it over and dumped it out.

Spread out across the table were trinkets and toys and stuff a much younger girl might enjoy. Again Kate wanted to say it wasn't her bag, but how would she ever explain where hers was? And if she did produce it, her radio watches would be proof enough that they were spies.

The Geists were smooth, all right, probably spilling the one container in Boise on purpose to show that they were carrying seeds. And asking to sit in the back so they could keep an eye on the cargo and get the food prepared, all the while switching tags on the luggage. When exactly had they put the ID tags on the cargo containers? Even more curious, had they found old tags or created phony ones?

"Well," Dad said, "you can believe what you want and I know you will do what you want, but I would like to go on record that we have been royally framed by Howard and June Geist of Boise, Idaho. I hope someday they come to justice."

"Señor Michaels," General Valdez said with a tired sigh, "do you think I know no German?"

"German?"

"Yes, do you know any?"

"Not really."

"Surely you know the meaning of the word *geist* in German."

"Can't say that I do," Dad said.

"Ghost, sir. It means ghost. You and I both know that the Geists are a figment of your imagination. They do not exist, and you cannot pin this on them."

The Escape

Kate had never felt so terrified. She remembered her fear and grief when her mother died. And then there was the plane crash in the jungles of Indonesia. But to hear that her father would be put to death, especially for something he didn't do, and that she and her brother would be sent to live in an orphanage in the middle of nowhere—well, that was too much.

Kate thought her heart would burst. She wanted to grab onto her dad and never let go, and she could see Chad felt the same. What were they going to do? She sneaked a peek at Eva Flores. The woman stared at the floor.

Valdez called on a soldier to search the three yet again and empty their pockets onto the table. Dad stared meaningfully at Kate as she was searched, and he let out a huge sigh when his wallet did not turn up. Clearly he was desperate to know where it was, and Kate wanted badly to tell him.

Chad surrendered his watch, a folded-up computer instruction book, his wallet with nine dollars and pictures of his friends and family, some change, and a key ring with the Yukon Do It logo on it. Valdez raised his eyebrows at Dad when he saw that. But Dad had fallen silent, and Kate wondered if he had just resigned himself to whatever came next.

Dad's pockets were empty, except for some change, a small pocketknife, and a key ring. Kate's pockets held only a couple of pieces of tissue paper and a loose bracelet.

"What were you going to do for money here in Branco Grande?" Valdez said.

Dad said nothing.

"You have hidden some money somewhere? Credit cards? Your identification?"

"You have my passport and visa."

"You see how this appears, Señor Michaels? It appears you were going to use cash from your weapons and drug sales to finance your stay here."

"As a matter of fact, this was an in and out mission. We planned to fly the Geists ... er ... the Kennicotts in, and then turn around and fly back."

"Again you insult me by lying to me? We knew the Kennicotts were coming because we invited them. We knew what they were bringing. They told us how they were getting here and we checked you out. We may be a new country, but we have computers and telephones. It was not hard to find that you had reservations at the Plaza del Rio, of which we are very proud. How were you going to pay for that?"

"We were staying only until Monday," Dad said. "Now I'm through answering your questions."

"All the more reason for me to sentence you here and now."

"I had some money and some credit cards. I'm sure if you search the plane carefully, you'll find them. Or maybe they fell out on the runway."

"I am through being toyed with, señor. I will confer with the other jurors and pronounce sentence."

Kate looked at her dad. Did he want her to tell these people where his wallet was? But what would that help? And if he wanted her to tell, he would say so. But maybe he was afraid she would be punished for having hidden it. What could they do to her? If she were going to lose her father anyway, she didn't much care what happened to her.

Eva Flores was growing more and more agitated. Kate could tell by the look in her eyes and how she rubbed her hands together. Finally, she spoke for the first time, with a tiny, fragile, but melodic voice. "General Valdez, sir, should I not take the children to the toilet before you announce —"

"No! Let them stay! We will determine what to do with them now too."

Dad spoke up. "Sir, let me appeal to your sense of decency. Do you have children?"

"That is none of your business."

"Then you must. Would you want them present when you were sentenced, guilty or not? I beg you not to put them through this ordeal."

Valdez pressed his lips together and appeared frustrated. Eva Flores leaned toward him, pleading with her eyes. Finally he waved her off. "Take them!" he said. "But have them back here in twenty minutes."

"I want to stay," Chad said quickly.

"Me too," Kate said, but Eva looked stricken and shook her head slightly at Kate.

"No, let's go." Eva came around the table to round them up.

"Go, kids," Dad said. "Please. I don't want you to hear this."

"But I may never see you again!" Chad shouted.

"You'll let me say good-bye to them, won't you, sir?" Dad said.

Valdez turned away from his associates. "Yes, of course. Now go!"

Eva hurried from the room, and Chad and Kate followed her down the hall. She herded them into a small waiting room where Kate could see out the window that the sun had begun to set. It was still hot.

"How do they execute people in this country?" Chad said.

Eva looked at him as if she knew she could not evade the question. "Firing squad."

Kate swallowed a whimper. "Do they do it right away?"

"No. Usually thirty days. I don't know why they wait. Nothing ever changes."

"What do you think my dad will get?" Chad said.

Eva looked away and shook her head.

"You think they'll shoot him?"

"I've seen people shot for less."

"My dad is innocent, you know," Kate said.

"Is he?" Eva said, not unkindly. "Tell me."

"Everything he said is true. He's never done a thing wrong in his life! He would never do anything like this." Kate paused, wanting to sound grown up. "Those people told us they were the Geists, and we gave them a free flight down here to deliver the medicine and seeds. I had a feeling something wasn't right about them, and I was right."

"You had a feeling?" Eva said.

"Yeah," Chad grumbled. "She's got women's intuition. Lot of good it'll do us now."

"But everything I just told you is true," Kate said.

"That's right," Chad said. "Dad is completely innocent."

Eva opened the door an inch and looked down the hallway. "I too have intuition," she whispered. "But this time it's more than a feeling. I'm going to tell you why I believe you."

"You believe us?" Kate said. "Why didn't you say so? Why don't you tell the general?"

"I have no say there," she said. "No say."

"Then why are you in there?"

"I'm on his staff, that's all I'll say. But I have seen too much killing. Too much so-called justice. I can't stand by and see a family torn apart like this."

"What can you do?"

"I can show you how to get out of here, but he'll be asking for you in about fifteen minutes. Maybe I can stall another five. I'll say you pushed me down and got away. If he knows I helped you escape, I'll be killed."

Kate glanced at Chad. Could they really leave their dad behind? Did they have any choice? "But why do you believe us?" Kate said.

"The Kennicotts," she said. "I've seen them before. They are friends of the general. What they brought in, they brought in for him."

"Then why didn't they just unload it without us knowing about it and let us go?" Chad said.

"Paco is new. He was not informed. He was not supposed to find anything in your luggage. We would have checked you out at the Plaza del Rio and made sure you weren't international agents. If it looked like you were going to expose the general, you would have been in trouble. Otherwise, you would have been on your way."

"If you can get us out of here, where would we go?" Chad said.

The woman leaned close and continued in a whisper. "I cannot tell you where to go. I would love to give you sanctuary, but there is no way I can do that without someone telling the general. Don't trust anyone in this city or in this country. If you can get to Santiago or to Buenos Aires, you can probably call back to your own country. Get as far from here as you can."

"We can't leave our father," Kate said. "Where will they keep him?"

"The central prison is downtown, about four blocks from the Plaza del Rio. It's an awful place. Awful. You wouldn't want to see it."

"How can we get our dad out of there?"

"You have to get help for him within thirty days or there will be no hope."

"Then get us out of here," Chad said.

"Here's what we'll do," she said. "I am going to take each of you to the bathroom. When there is no one else in either of the bathrooms, lock both doors from the inside." She pointed at Chad. "Kick out the little door under the sink that leads to the pipes. You can squeeze through there until you're in the women's bathroom. That bathroom has a window that opens to the back of the building. Go straight away from the building and no one will see you. It's about five miles to the city, and by the time you get there, your descriptions will have been sent everywhere. You will stand out with your blond hair and green eyes, so stay out of sight."

"But what—"

"I don't know what else to tell you or how to help you," she said. "And you must hurry."

"Wait," Chad said. "I've got an idea that will give us more time. You come into the bathroom with me and lie on the floor as if we knocked you out. They'll have to break the door down to get in, and they'll find you on the floor, that hole kicked in the wall, and the open window in the other bathroom. But by then we'll be long gone."

"That *will* help me," Eva said. "I will look silly being overtaken by children, but I am a good actress."

Her legs trembling, Kate went into the women's washroom and locked the door. In the mirror she saw a girl so pale, with eyes so huge, that she hardly recognized herself.

Through the thin walls, she could hear Chad talking quickly to Eva. "What are common names for kids in this town?"

"Oh, something like Manuel or Manny for you. Conchita for her."

"Can you do us one more favor? Can you get us some hair dye?"

Eva paused. "Maybe."

"Leave it at the counter at the Plaza del Rio. Tell 'em it's for Manny and Conchita."

"You shouldn't go there! They'll look for you, knowing you had reservations."

"I'll figure out something," Chad said. "Just leave it there and we'll find a way to get it."

Kate jumped back when the thin wood wall broke through and Chad climbed into her bathroom. Kate squatted to look for Eva, who peeked through and reached in to take both of Kate's hands. "God go with you," Eva said.

Chad was already climbing through the window. Kate caught up and whispered for him to wait.

"What for? We've got to go! Somehow I've got to call Uncle Bill in Portland."

"Chad! I hid Dad's wallet in that one jeep. My backpack, too, with our wrist TVs and other stuff."

"Great! And we'll need hats until we can get our hair dyed."

"I've got a terry-cloth cap and a sun visor in there."

"How can we get it?"

"We've got to find the jeep with the broken headlight and the crunched front bumper."

"Okay. And then we've got to go, Kate."

She hesitated at the thought of leaving their dad. "I know."

They each climbed through the window and held onto the window sill before dropping to the ground. Then they split up and ran to either end of the building, where they peeked around the side into the gathering darkness. If the jeep was still parked where the men had left it, Kate would be closest. She would make a dash to get the stuff and meet Chad in the back again.

But when Kate got to her end of the building and looked around front, her heart sank. The jeep was gone. She looked back at Chad, who waved at her to come to his end. She could barely see him. That meant no one else could easily see them either. She sprinted to him.

"Look," he said. Six jeeps were parked side by side in front of a metal Quonset hut. "It has to be one of those, doesn't it?"

"Probably, but they all look alike from behind."

"You take one end, and I'll take the other," Chad said. They raced into the darkness. They tried to tiptoe quietly across a patch of gravel, but then they were on asphalt

again, and their steps were silent. Kate ran to one end of
the line of jeeps, and Chad ran to the other. Chad found the
right vehicle, second from the end.

"Here!" he cried softly, and Kate ran to the other end.
She pointed under the seat, and Chad pulled her backpack
out while she yanked the wallet out from its hiding place.
Then they ran off into the darkness.

As they ran Kate finally began to feel the fatigue from
the short, restless night the night before, then the long trip,
the short nap, the terror, and now the escape. She knew
Chad would not slow down until they were a long way from
the terminal. She considered herself lucky that she had
nothing to carry but the wallet.

And they kept running.

Finding Shelter

"Man, your backpack is heavy!" Chad shouted, panting. "What have you got in there?"

"Lots of stuff," Kate said between gasps. "It probably just feels heavy because you're running and tired."

"Then you carry it for a while."

Chad let the strap slip off his shoulder and caught it in one hand. He slowed enough to allow Kate to catch up, then slung the pack to her. It nearly knocked her over.

"Whoa!" She stumbled and tried to keep running. She handed him Dad's wallet and struggled with the backpack. "This *is* heavy! I've got to rest, Chad!"

"Let's make it to the trees first!"

They slowed to a jog and often looked behind them. There was no activity at the airstrip, at least from what they could tell in the darkness. The lights on either side of the one long runway would have silhouetted anyone running toward them from that direction. They were about a quarter of a mile from a thick cluster of trees.

Kate finally slowed to a walk, shifted the backpack from one shoulder to the other, then slipped both arms under the straps so it lay flat on her back. That made it a little easier to carry, but she could tell there was more inside than she had packed.

Chad was the first to flop to the ground when they reached the trees. "No one can see us here," he said.

Kate joined him. "What do you think they'll do to Dad when they find us missing?"

"We can't worry about that. It's out of our control." Chad leaned against a tree. "Let's rest and then walk to town." He pointed right.

Kate saw faint city lights in the sky. "That's not much light for a capital city. How far do you figure that is?"

"Eva said five miles from the airport, but I'd say it's farther than that."

"Even five miles is too far," Kate said, her heart still banging and her breath coming in short bursts. "I'm thirsty."

"There's no water around here and anything we find in Branco Grande, unless it's bottled or from a well, will probably make us sick."

"Oh, great." Kate fought tears. "Where will we find help?"

"The police could be as crooked as the general." Chad shook his head. "Somehow we've got to get a call through to Uncle Bill. He'll know what we should do."

Kate leaned back, pressing the backpack against a tree, and sucked in a huge breath. She looked at the sky. The stars were just coming into view, and the temperature was dropping fast. Her skin was cold, but her body still felt warm from all the running. Half a minute later, however, she started to shiver. She slid out from under the backpack, untied the sweater from around her waist, and pulled it on.

She wrestled the backpack into her lap. "I wish I could see enough to tell what's in this," she said.

"Yeah," Chad said. "Wish we had a flashlight."

Kate dug into the bag. "Oh, no!" she whispered. "Oh, my goodness! Chad!"

"What?" She handed him a huge pistol. "Whoa!" he said. "Man, I wonder if this thing is loaded!"

"Be careful, just in case. Oh, Chad! Here's another one!"

"Make sure you keep the barrel pointed away from me," he said. "What else is in there?"

Kate set the handgun on the ground and pawed through the bag. "Our wrist TVs are here. And the hat and the sun visor." She found a small but heavy cardboard box stuck down in the corner. She pulled it out. "What do you think this is?" she said, handing it to Chad.

"Bullets," he said. "Too heavy to be anything else."

"And this?" She handed him a floppy plastic bag with something loose and shifting in it.

"Oh, no," he said. "This feels like those bags of drugs the general found in Dad's and my backpacks."

"And in the pack that had my name on it," Kate said. "Shouldn't we get rid of the guns and the drugs?"

"I don't know," Chad said. "They're evidence. Kate, we'd better keep moving."

They repacked the bag, then Chad handed the wallet back to Kate and hoisted the pack onto his back. She peered back at the airstrip a mile away. Nothing. By now someone should have come looking for them and found Eva Flores on the bathroom floor. Kate hoped Eva was as good an actress as she thought she was. The last thing Kate wanted was for Eva to get in trouble over their escape. No matter what happened, they owed a lot to that brave woman.

They started off again, Chad moving quickly, even with the heavy pack on his back. The ground became less even, and Kate felt dust puffing up almost to her knees with every heel-dragging step. She was exhausted and wanted to sleep.

"What are we going to do when we get to the city?" she said.

"No idea," Chad said. "I want to look for a place where we can stop and I can see what else is in the backpack. And we need a place to sleep. In the morning we need to find that hotel, get the hair dye, and see if we can make a call to the States."

They trudged on. Despite the cool breeze in her face, Kate felt her body warming again. She was perspiring, but she didn't want to go to the trouble of taking off her sweater and tying it around her waist. Tired and miserable as she felt, she just wanted to keep going.

An hour later they came to the outskirts of the capital of Amazonia, Branco Grande. From what she had seen in the hotel brochure, she expected a huge, modern city. This was strange. A single neon sign glowed in the night sky, and as she and her brother carefully maneuvered through alleys and back streets, they got close enough to read it. Sure enough, it was the Branco Grande Plaza del Rio. Chad chuckled.

"What's funny?" Kate said.

"Besides the fact that the hotel is the only modern building in this town? I just figured out what it means in English. It's the Big Horse Place of the River."

Kate smiled, but she was too tired to laugh. Anyway, she kept wondering what was happening to Dad. What was the general doing to him? Was he even alive?

The hotel sign was the brightest thing around. Only about a third of the street lights were lit. So far, they had seen no one. Then they heard voices from a few streets away.

They stayed in the shadows and circled around the back
of the unpaved road that separated the city from the desert.
Several hundred yards away sat a small gathering of adobe-type
buildings with vehicles parked outside. A light burned in one of
the windows, and a single bare bulb hung in what looked like a
combination garage and stable attached to the lighted building.

"We might be able to hide in there and even sleep," Chad
said. "Come on."

Kate felt like a robot, but somehow she forced her legs
onward. When they got within the ring of light from the
bulb at the end of the larger building, Chad let the backpack slip off his shoulders and set it on the ground.

"Is that a well?" Kate said, pointing to a small structure
nearby. Her throat was parched.

"Yeah, wait here," Chad said.

"Be careful. There's got to be people in there."

She watched as Chad crept around the other side of
the building in the darkness, then came around again and
peeked in the window of the tiny house attached to the
stable. She held her breath and prayed no one would see or
hear him. He ducked quickly away from the window and
scampered back around the buildings toward the well. Then
he slowly and quietly lowered and raised the bucket. He
untied it and carried it to Kate and they both drank. Kate
had never tasted water so sweet and refreshing.

"There are a bunch of guys in there," he told her, "most of them with their shirts off like they're ready for bed. They're eating and drinking and playing cards, and there are bunk beds crammed in there. The name on the building is the same as the one on the sides of those trucks and jeeps. So they must work for this company and live here."

"What's in the garage?"

"One old truck or tractor or something, a cow, and a couple of goats. The goats are in a pen, and the cow is tied to the wall. There's room enough in there for us to sleep."

"But what if they find us?"

"I don't want to think about it."

"Shouldn't we at least wait until they're all asleep?"

"Probably," Chad said. "I'm going to take the bucket back over there, then let's just sit here awhile."

They watched for an hour, Kate dozing and rousing every time she heard a car or truck in the distance. "It's nothing," Chad would say as they sat in the shadows. "No one can see us here."

Finally he nudged her awake. "The light just went off where they were playing cards," he said.

She stood, dizzy and disoriented. "Chad, I'm so tired. I have to lie down."

"Me too," he said. "Let's sneak into the stable, but be quiet. They won't be sound asleep for quite a while."

As they crept out of the shadows and down the street,
a noisy window fan came on in the bunkhouse. "That's
good," Chad whispered. "They won't hear anything, but we
still have to be careful."

Just then the door swung open. A young man in a flannel shirt came out and headed for the well. Kate and Chad
stopped. Kate held her breath and couldn't hear Chad breath-
ing either. They were out in the open but still in the dark.

The young man grabbed the bucket, but it quickly came
loose of the rope, and he nearly dropped it down the well.
He muttered something angrily in his own language, then
looked around. He retied the rope to the bucket, drew some
water, and headed for the stable.

Kate let her breath out. "I hope he's not sleeping in
there," she whispered.

They heard noises from the stable, as if the man was
watering the animals. Soon he returned the bucket, padded
back to the bunkhouse, and slammed the door. Kate and
Chad waited a few more minutes, then tiptoed to the stable.

The big wood door was open only about three inches.
Since Chad was carrying the heavy backpack, Kate put
Dad's wallet in her waistband and pushed on the door with
both hands. It creaked loudly, so she stopped and tried
again. It made noise each time, but she stayed with it until it
was open enough for them to squeeze through.

Kate could hardly stomach the stench, but she knew they didn't have any choice. It would be cold enough inside; she didn't want to think about sleeping outside. They stepped into the stable, but then the cow began to moo.

"Oh, no," Chad whispered. "Shh, moo cow," he said. "Shh!"

"She probably doesn't understand English," Kate whispered.

"Shh isn't English!" Chad said. "Be quiet-o, el cow-o!"

Kate laughed so hard she had to cover her mouth. But what if the workers heard the cow and came to investigate? Chad and Kate looked at each other in the sliver of light coming from the bulb outside. They stood still and silent, and suddenly the cow turned away and fell quiet.

Kate touched Chad's arm and pointed. A makeshift ladder of planks nailed to the wall led to a tiny hayloft about eight feet overhead. She couldn't see much hay up there, but at least they would be out of sight in case someone came in.

"Let me get started up there, and then hand me the backpack," Chad whispered.

He climbed a few steps, then held on with one hand and reached with the other for the pack. Kate lifted it over her head in both hands and felt the pain in her shoulders and upper arms. When Chad grabbed it, it nearly swung him off his perch.

"Whoa!" he whispered.

Chad tried to swing the backpack into the loft ahead of him, but it was too heavy and kept pulling him away from the wall. The cow turned to stare at them, and the goats in the pen stirred and stood.

"You're going to have to push," Chad said.

Kate made sure Dad's wallet was secure at her waist and then started up the ladder. The planks were nailed flat against the wall and didn't angle out away from the wall like a normal ladder, so it was harder to climb. She didn't think she could climb with only one arm.

Kate moved slowly up the ladder to just below where Chad stood. She planted her feet and held on with her left hand, then pushed on the backpack with her right, and Chad was able to go up one more rung. Then she had to grab with both hands again to keep her balance. They did this for every rung until Chad finally curled his left arm around a vertical plank on the floor of the loft. Kate gave one last push and the backpack tumbled into the hayloft, the guns inside thudding against the wood.

Chad helped Kate the rest of the way up.

"What now?" she said, almost passing out from the fatigue.

"I was just wondering what the cow and goats would think if one of those guns went off!"

Kate collapsed into a heap. "It wouldn't make much difference what the animals thought. The guys inside would sure come running."

"We'd hold them off with the guns," Chad said.

Kate was too tired to respond. She knew he was kidding, and it was supposed to be funny, but she didn't have the energy to laugh. They should never have come on this trip in the first place. Why hadn't her dad or Chad listened to her?

Moonlight shown through a two-foot-square opening in the wall. "Let me see Dad's wallet," Chad said. While he held it up to the light, Kate began pulling stuff out of her backpack. She left the guns inside. Chad had been right; the heavy little box contained, according to the label, twenty bullets for a nine-millimeter Luger. She pulled out the heavy plastic bag filled with powder.

"This looks darker than the stuff in the other bags, doesn't it?"

Chad looked at it. "Yeah. It looks brown, but maybe it's just too dark in here to tell."

"Looks brown to me," she said. "Like wheat flour. Maybe it's not drugs at all."

"Kate," Chad said slowly and dramatically. "Do you know what Dad has in his wallet?"

"Money and travelers checks and credit cards, I suppose."

"Right. Of course, the travelers checks and the credit cards won't do us any good, because we can't match his signature and no one would accept them from kids anyway. But Kate, Dad's got fifty twenty-dollar bills in here."

Kate calculated silently. "A thousand dollars? What for?"

"I don't know. Emergencies, I guess."

"Well, they don't use American dollars here anyway, do they?"

"Actually, American dollars are valuable everywhere. In fact, in a lot of places they're illegal because they're worth so much. If you get caught using American currency in some European countries, you can be in big trouble. They probably use some sort of Argentinean or Chilean money here. I wouldn't think they'd have their own currency yet. But American dollars have to be like gold."

"We'll find out," Kate said. "We're not going to get far without paying somebody something, are we?"

"That's for sure. Let me see those hats."

Kate pulled out the floppy terry-cloth cap and the sun visor.

"If you put your hair up and stuffed it into this one, would it hide it?" Chad said.

Kate used both hands to push her hair up, then held it in place as Chad plopped the floppy hat on her head. Blond curls peeked out from underneath. "Not too good," he said, as he put the sun visor on. "What do you think?"

"There's no hiding it," Kate said. "You look like a blond American boy wearing a visor."

"Let's hope Eva leaves some dye for us," Chad said.

But Kate did more than hope. As she curled up in the hay, shoulders hunched against the cold, she prayed as she always did before sleeping. But this time it was without Dad there. She prayed for him and she prayed for Chad. She prayed for herself. And while the prickly hay and the hard floor made the most uncomfortable bed she could remember since the jungles of Indonesia, she finally fell asleep.

She awoke when Chad turned in his sleep and kicked her. She had no idea what time it was, but the loft was stifling from the early morning sun. As she sat up and squinted against the harsh light streaming through the cracks in the walls, she heard footsteps below. She lay back down and silently rolled onto her side so she could peek through the crack in the floor. The cow was gone, and she watched a young man close the goat pen. The goats scooted out, and then something seemed to catch the man's attention. He looked up, as if staring straight into Kate's eyes.

He looked puzzled and moved toward the ladder. The backpack! One of the straps hung over the side, and he was coming to investigate. He climbed two steps and reached to grab the strap. Kate rolled quickly and wrapped the backpack in her arms, burying her face in it. She kicked

Chad hard and he sat up. She put one finger to her lips and pointed downward.

She felt a yank as the young man continued to pull on the backpack. He was strong, and she had to hook her feet around a sturdy post to hang on. He would discover them, there was no doubt of that. But she would not let him have their stuff without a fight.

The young man yanked on the strap again, and Kate grimaced and hung on with all her might. As the bag pulled her closer to the edge, she stiffened and tightened her feet in a desperate attempt to hang on to the post.

By now Chad had stuffed Dad's wallet into his pocket, bent over Kate, and grabbed the backpack. Kate hung on even tighter. Now it was their four young arms against the muscular laborer in a tug of war that could cost them their lives.

Close Calls

Kate grunted as the young man in the flannel shirt pulled on the other end of the backpack strap. She peeked around the bag and peered down at the Amazonian. He hung from the backpack with his toes barely touching one of the ladder planks. Kate and Chad were tugging against his entire weight.

Suddenly his feet slipped off the plank. "Left!" she shouted, and Chad pulled and jerked the bag a few inches. The young man held on and was yanked away from the ladder.

Success! His feet slipped free and he dangled a couple of feet off the ground. But now Kate heard threads popping on the backpack as the young man's weight strained the straps. She and Chad were wedged together, arms enveloping the bag. They would have the advantage if they could hold out only a few seconds more.

Kate rocked, which caused the man to swing, and finally he lost his grip. He shrieked as he toppled onto the hard dirt floor, his seat smacking, the back of his head banging, and his feet flying over his head. Kate and Chad watched him somersault into the door of the goat pen, which slammed shut so hard that it flew back and hit him again, knocking him flat onto his stomach.

He lay there shaking his head as if to make the world stop spinning, but Kate knew they couldn't take any time to see if he was hurt. She jumped to her feet and started down the ladder.

"No!" Chad shouted. "You'll never get past him. C'mon! We have to jump!"

Chad slung the backpack out the opening in the wall, turned around and slid out. He hung by his hands, and when he was fully stretched out, he dropped the rest of the way to the ground.

Kate stepped into the opening. Eight feet looked like a long way down! Chad gathered up the backpack while she tried to decide how best to get down. She heard a bang on the floor behind her and whirled to see both hands of the young man grabbing the boards. He wasn't even going to try the ladder this time. He swung up with the toes of one booted foot and struggled to pull himself into the loft. But before he could get his other leg up, Kate ran over and kicked his foot off the ledge.

"Ayeee!" the young man shouted as he swung back down. He landed again on his seat and somersaulted back into the goat-pen door. Kate was afraid she might have killed him, but when she peeked down, he just lay there as if he had given up. She stepped through the opening and hung there, and Chad reached up to put a hand under each foot. They had never practiced anything like that, and soon she had fallen onto him. Immediately they scrambled to their feet.

"Let's go!" Chad said.

They ran, the backpack hanging between them, each holding one of the straps. Kate looked back to see the young man watching them from the hole in the hayloft.

They ran as fast as they could. Kate looked back as the young man hung by his hands and then dropped the rest of the way to the ground.

"He's coming!" she shouted.

Kate guessed he twisted his ankle, because he staggered and smacked into the well, finally tumbling to the ground. Kate and Chad raced away in the morning sunlight.

Branco Grande seemed bigger in the daylight, but it was still a dusty, crowded place that looked half-finished. Kate knew people would by now be on the lookout for the two blond kids who had escaped from the guards at the airport. For all she knew, there might even be a reward for finding them.

What a way to start a day! She was warm again but realized she wasn't wearing her sweater. "Oh, no! Chad, I left my sweater in that barn!"

"Big deal! You can get another one."

"Yeah, but it's evidence. It proves we were there and that we're probably here in town. I feel like everybody is looking at me and knows who I am."

"Nobody's looking at you," Chad said.

"They will be. We'd better stay out of sight or do something about our looks, and right now."

Kate and Chad stayed in the alleys and side streets, crossing any time they saw anyone who might pass them. Finally they came upon the worst part of town, where drunks slept in the street and little bands of people hung around. Some drank. Some smoked. Most just talked and laughed among themselves. These people, Kate guessed, were probably the type who wouldn't ask any questions because they didn't want any asked of them.

Still, she and Chad stayed in the shadows. While these people might not turn them in, they might want to steal anything they had of value. And to save Dad they needed everything in that backpack — including those guns.

"I need a bath," Kate said, squatting in the cool shade of a tree.

"You and me both," Chad said. "But first, we need clothes."

"A woman over there is selling clothes out of a cart. Should we see what she's got?"

Chad nodded, but Kate suddenly grabbed Chad's arm and pulled him behind a tree. "Look! A jeep from the airport!"

He peered around the trunk. "How do you know that's where it's from?"

"Paco's driving! Maybe the general sent him to look for us."

"Maybe." Chad shaded his eyes. "He's got a couple of other soldiers with him. I wonder if they're going to do a house-to-house search."

"Yeah," Kate said, "and I wonder if they've already been to that place where we slept. If they have, they know we're here."

Kate and Chad waited until the jeep turned toward the center of town before moving again. They crossed the street to where the old peasant woman had her used-clothing stand.

"We'd better not be seen together until we get some disguises," Chad said, and Kate nodded. "Wait over there," he added as he dug the floppy, white terry-cloth hat from the backpack. He jammed it down over his head.

Kate watched from a nearby alley as Chad approached the old woman's stand. The woman looked at him warily as he picked through her racks of hung clothes and her table of folded stuff. Then he spoke to her, and she quickly looked in every direction before leaning close to him, nodding and whispering. She reached behind the cart and slapped two pairs of sandals onto the table. Then she slid two pairs of long pants from the middle of a pile and laid them out beside the sandals. Then two button-type shirts, the least colorful of the ones she had. Chad asked her something else, and she dug around in a box, finally pulling out several caps and hats.

Once Chad seemed to have everything he needed, he turned his back to her and carefully pulled out one of the American twenty-dollar bills. When he turned back and offered it to her, she grabbed her heart. Again she looked this way and that and tried to explain something to him. He waved her off, and she clutched the bill to her heart.

Suddenly Kate heard the roar of an engine. She froze when it stopped behind her. Had they been discovered? Was it Paco and his compatriots?

A man directly behind her spoke out, "Pardon, señorita!"

She jumped and turned slowly, only to discover that she was merely in the man's way. He was picking up trash. Kate decided that a heart attack could not feel much worse than the way her chest felt right then. She looked into the street. Chad was jogging toward her in that stupid-looking hat, his

bundle of clothes and sandals under one arm. Behind him
the woman was packing up her stuff and preparing to move
her stand. The twenty American dollars must have been
more than she usually made in a week.

Kate and Chad ran off to the shady area of a rundown
park where Chad relayed what had gone on with the woman.

"She hardly understood English," he said. "I asked if she
took American dollars, and she just about went ballistic
on me. She looked around to see if anybody was watching,
and then she said something about no change. I figured she
meant she couldn't break a large bill. I said that was okay,
and then I started asking for shoes and hats, besides the
shirts and pants I found."

"Everybody around here seems to dress colorfully," Kate
said. "These look pretty drab. Will we blend in?"

"The people in this area dress plainer," Chad said,
"because they're obviously poorer. I think we need to look
like peasant kids, don't you?"

"I guess."

"Put this stuff on over your clothes, and later, when we
find a place to wash up, we can wear just the new stuff."

"The new *old* stuff, you mean? These are rags."

"Yeah, but at least they're clean."

Kate and Chad put their shoes into the backpack, which
was now heavier than ever, and put the big, baggy peasant

clothes on. They laughed when they looked at each other in the huge, wide-brimmed sombrero-type hats and thick-soled sandals.

"Now we don't have to split up," Kate said. "No one can see our hair or our pink skin."

"Yeah, unless they look at our hands and feet. Listen, Kate, we're going to have to take a risk if we want to get anywhere. One of us will have to go into the Plaza del Rio Hotel and ask if anyone left anything there for us, or we'll have to pay somebody to do it."

Kate nodded. "Chad, what did you say the name of that hotel means in English?"

"I was just guessing, but Branco sounds like bronco, which is a horse. Grande means big. Plaza is place, I think, and Rio means river."

"You think the hotel is really on a river?"

"Maybe. At least the brochure showed a fountain in the plaza."

"I wouldn't mind taking a bath in that fountain," Kate said, "but I don't suppose I'd ever get away with that."

"No way," Chad said, "but we should be able to follow the river out of town until we find a place where we can get cleaned up."

"I'm sure getting hungry."

"Me too. Let's see what we can find on the way."

They moved toward the center of town and saw the big hotel and the plaza in the distance.

"The river runs along behind it," Kate said, "just past that boulevard. See?"

"Yeah. Let's not get too close to the hotel yet. Let's just circle back and follow the river."

A man was selling roasted corn on the cob at a little stand on a street corner near the edge of town. It was Kate's turn to do the bargaining. She left Chad with the backpack and the wallet and shoved a twenty-dollar bill into her pocket.

"You've got to try to get change," Chad said. "If we keep spending American twenty-dollar bills all over town, we won't stay under cover for long."

Kate approached the man. "Speak English?" she said.

He held up his thumb and finger a half-inch apart.

"A little?"

He nodded, but so far she hadn't heard any of it.

"Take American dollars?" she said.

He nodded vigorously, but looked up and down the street, the same way the clothes lady had.

"Four corn." Kate held up four fingers and pointed to the cobs.

The man quickly took four sharp sticks and stabbed the cobs.

"How much?" She looked hungrily at the corn.

"One American dollar," he said slowly.

"One?"

He nodded.

"Change?" she said. "Change for twenty?"

"Twenty?" He shrugged. "Twenty okay!"

"No!" she said. "Need change!"

He squatted next to a cigar box and opened it. It was full of local currency—bills and coins. He pointed to the box and then to Kate. "Change, twenty," he said.

She had no idea how much the change was worth, but she took all he had, and the corn, and gave him the twenty. The man immediately began closing up his cart. *He"s probably going off to buy a house*, Kate thought.

"Sir?" she said. "Can you tell me where the prison is?"

"Prison?" His eyes narrowed.

She nodded, hoping he wouldn't report her.

He pointed down the street. Just as Eva had said, about four blocks this side of the Plaza del Rio stood a block-long complex. Her heart ached; Dad was probably in that prison. Had he already been tortured and beaten—or worse?

The Plaza del Rio

When Kate pointed out the prison to Chad, he stopped and stared. She understood his look. It didn't look like a prison at all. The structure was as long and wide as a whole city block and made of adobe and wood beams. As they got closer they saw bars on openings in the walls; the place was obviously built for some other purpose and then converted into a prison.

People could walk right by the prison, and though heavily armed guards hung around and could have shot anyone trying to escape, the whole thing looked pretty casual.

"We'll look obvious with this backpack, even in these clothes," Chad said. He suggested they hurry past the prison on the other side of the street and head out of town to the river, where they could wash up. Then he tucked the backpack under his huge shirt, and they made their way down the street.

Kate was nearly overcome by the smell as they walked past the prison. It was worse than the smell in the barn the night before. "What *is* that?" she wondered aloud.

"Smells like they don't have any plumbing," Chad said. "Yuck!"

"You think Dad's in there?"

"I hope not."

"If he is, we've got to get him out of there."

They were nearly a block past the prison when Kate whirled around. "Chad, look!"

It was Paco again, slowly driving a jeep past the prison. The young man who had almost caught Kate and Chad that morning sat beside Paco in the front seat. Tied around his neck was Kate's sweater.

"Let's get out of here!" Kate said.

Kate and Chad darted down an alley, circled around the prison, and kept running until they were about a mile outside of town. "Did you see what I saw?" Chad asked when they slowed. "At the back side of the prison?"

"What?"

"All those little kids crowded around the windows."

"No, I didn't."

"If we can dye our hair and somehow keep from looking so light-skinned," Chad said, "we can blend in with those kids. The guards were right there, but it looked like the kids were talking to the prisoners, maybe even selling them something."

"Let's check that out," Kate said.

No one was around, and the river looked clean and inviting in the heat. They were both surprised at how cold it was. They washed quickly and put on their new South American clothes. Then it was off to the Plaza del Rio to see if Eva Flores had left them any hair dye.

"How are we going to get in there?" Kate said. "You know they'll be watching for us."

Chad nodded. "We've got to keep the backpack out of sight. In fact, maybe we should get some kind of a new bag."

"I like this bag!"

"But it could get us caught."

On their way back into town, this time circling wide of the prison, Kate and Chad came upon a small storefront where leather goods were sold.

"I'll hang onto the backpack," Chad said. "See if you can get a leather bag with the change you got from the corn guy."

Kate entered and looked around. Despite her clothes and the hat hiding her hair, there was no pretending she was South American. A woman approached and said, "Español?"

Kate shook her head. "English."

"Okay," the woman said, but she did not seem comfortable with that.

"Leather bag?" Kate said.

The woman looked puzzled and shook her head. Kate pointed to a big leather bag on a high shelf. "Oh, bueno," the woman said, and used a long pole to pull it down. Kate put the strap over her shoulder and smiled.

"How much?"

"Much?"

Kate made a gesture with her thumb and fingers. The woman responded in Spanish. Kate didn't understand. She produced the change she had in local currency, which she hoped totaled more than fifteen dollars in American money.

The woman took it and carefully counted it out. "No," she said. "No. More."

Kate held up one finger to tell her to wait, left the bag, and hurried out to Chad. "Let me have another twenty," she said.

Back in the store the woman looked at the twenty, quickly folded it, and put it in her pocket. "Okay," she said, nodding. "Okay."

But Kate had learned. "Change." And she thrust out her hand. The woman shook her head, so Kate moved as if to give the bag back. The woman reached in another pocket, looked around, and then quickly gave Kate, of all things, five dollars change in American currency.

"We can use that," Chad said a few minutes later as they emptied the backpack into the leather bag. "I hate giving twenties to people who would be thrilled with five." Chad fingered the bag of brown powder that had been planted in Kate's backpack. "I still wonder what this is."

When they finally came into view of the hotel, Kate said, "We're still too obvious. We need to split up."

"Let's get someone to go to the desk in there and see if anything has been left for us," Chad said.

"How will we find someone who speaks English?"

"Lots of these people understand English," he said. "It must be their second language."

"Let's find a kid who wants a little money," Kate said.

"A bunch of kids are playing over near the fountain, but one of us should stay out of sight."

"I'll go," Kate said. "I'll find someone."

"When you do, offer them a little of that local change to get something in there that was left for Manny or Conchita."

Chad stayed on a bench near a small cluster of trees, while Kate slowly approached some children frolicking near a fountain in the plaza. "English?" she said. "Anybody speak English?"

The kids looked shyly at her. Some smiled, some scowled. None, it seemed, understood. She kept moving, speaking quietly. "English?"

Finally, a little girl smiled at her and pointed at an older boy. "José," she called out. "English. English."

"Sí," he said. "Yes. What?"

"You speak English?"

"A little. What you want, Yankee?"

"You want to earn some money, José?"

"Money?" He straightened his back and looked doubtfully at her.

Kate dug into her pocket and pulled out three bills of the local currency. She had no idea what they were worth. The boy's eyes lit up, but then he grew wary again.

"How I make money?"

"Just go into the hotel and ask at the desk for a delivery for Manny or Conchita."

"Manny or Conchita?"

"Yes."

"Why?"

"To earn the money, José."

"You give money first."

"No way, José."

Kate almost laughed, but José had apparently never heard that before.

"Who's Manny and Conchita?"

"Too many questions," Kate said, and she turned to leave.

"No. I do! I do! Ask for delivery."

"Right."

"Okay, Yankee."

José ran toward the front of the Plaza del Rio, but before Kate could see whether he had moved all the way inside, she heard, "Conchita! Conchita!"

She spun and saw Chad waving frantically at her from the shadow of the trees. "Run, Conchita! Run!"

Kate wanted to wait for José and get the hair dye, but Chad wasn't the type to get excited over nothing. She jogged toward him, but he waved all the harder, so she began sprinting. Before she reached him, he began running too. She knew she could never catch him unless he let her, so she just followed him. They ran down one street after another, through alleys, and eventually came to the poorer section of town again.

Finally Chad slowed and stopped behind a brick building. Kate reached him and dropped to the ground, panting. "What's up?" she said. "I found a kid and he's in there getting the package. What's wrong?"

"The Geists," Chad said, sucking for air. "They weren't a hundred feet from you. They parked a small car in front of the hotel and stood there looking all around before they hurried in. I thought for sure they'd seen you. They were staring right at you. I waited until they went inside before I called you. If they're friends of General Valdez, they'll tell him where we are."

"But now what do we do about the dye? If José has it, he'll think I was a liar and won't have any idea what I was up to. What if he throws it away?"

"He wouldn't do that. He might sell it, though." Chad hoisted the leather bag to his shoulder. "We've still got to try to get it."

"I'm going to go back and find him." Kate scooped some dust and dirt into her hands, clapped, and then rubbed her feet and ankles. She did the same to her face. "Is it working?"

"Is what working? You look dirty, if that's what you wanted."

"I just don't want to look so white."

"It's working. You look like a dirty American. Kate, be careful. If you see the Geists, don't let them see you, whatever you do."

Kate wasn't so sure about being this far from Chad. What if one of them got caught? The other would be left to fend for herself or himself. Since Chad was staying with the big leather bag, the guns, and what they thought might be drugs, she would get out their wrist TVs and see if they worked from that far away.

From three blocks away, Kate could still hear Chad and even see a faint image of him on the tiny TV screen.

"This is too cool," he said. "But I probably shouldn't talk to you when people are around and can hear the static."

"Right," she said. "And don't let anyone see it. Keep it tucked up under your sleeve."

Kate felt a lot better now that she knew she could call Chad for help, and it also gave her an idea. If Dad was in the nearby prison, maybe they could somehow get a wrist TV in to him. If there were enough light, she could see him and he could see them. If he had any privacy at all, maybe he could tell them what to do.

When Kate got back to the plaza in front of the hotel, she kept an eye out for the Geists. But she soon realized that José was nowhere to be found. What must he have thought—a "Yankee" promises him money to do an errand and then runs away as fast as she can go?

"José?" she asked the children in the area. "José?"

They shrugged. Some frowned as if they knew she had promised him money and then run out on him.

Kate kept searching for José, then found a spot that was out of sight but still dangerously close to the hotel. She clicked the switch at the side of her wrist TV and whispered, "Chad, are you there?"

"I'm here," he said. "You okay?"

"I'm okay, but no José. Can you see me? I have no picture of you."

"Yeah, I can see you a little," he said. "Not too well."

"What kind of a car were the Geists driving, and where did they park?"

"It's a Japanese four-door, and they parked right in front of the hotel at the top of the circle drive."

"They're still there," Kate said.

"How do you know? Are you that close?"

"See for yourself," Kate said, and she held her wrist toward the front of the hotel.

"That's the car!" Chad said. "If it's red, that is."

"It is," Kate said.

"Then get away from there."

"They can't see me. I'm all right."

"You've got to find José."

"I know, but I don't know where to look. I'm thinking about going into the hotel myself and seeing whether he picked up the package."

"No! Don't risk it!"

Suddenly a voice from the shadows startled Kate. "Psst! Are you Conchita?"

Kate flinched and stared at José. She quickly dropped her arm so that her sleeve covered the wrist TV. "José!" she said, "I'm sorry I had to run off."

"Where you go?" he said.

"No questions," she said. "Did you get the package?"

"I got it." He patted his pocket. "How much?"

"I already told you." She reached into her pocket and pulled out the three local bills.

"Not enough," he said. "Could sell this for more."

"But it's not yours to sell," she told him.

"It is now."

"That would be stealing."

"How do I know you not steal it anyway? You no Conchita. You no even from here."

"How much do you want?"

"Want American dollars."

"I can give you five."

"Five American dollars?" he said. "Let me see!"

She found the five. He reached for it, but she pulled it back. "Give me the package first."

Suddenly José's eyes grew cold. He scowled at her. "I could break you into pieces," he said. "I could take all your money and keep your package."

Kate casually reached up under her sleeve and turned on her wrist TV. "I'm not alone," she said.

"What?" José said, looking around.

"My brother is here with me, and my father is in town too."

"I see nobody."

"If you listen closely, they will tell you you had better give me the package and take the five dollars and get away from me."

"Ha! I'm listening!"

From under her sleeve came Chad's low, gravelly voice as he tried to imitate an adult. "José! Give Conchita the package now, take the five dollars, and get away from her!"

José grabbed the paper bag from his pocket and tossed it to Kate, then dashed away.

"Your money!" she called after him, holding the five-dollar bill at her side so as not to make a scene.

José stopped and turned around. He eyed her carefully, then ran back and grabbed the five on his way past.

"I got it," Kate said into her wrist TV.

"Then get back here fast," Chad said. "What was that all about?"

"I'll tell you when I get there," she said, "but I want to check something out first."

Branco Grande Prison

Something about the Plaza del Rio had caught Kate's eye.
Their best hiding place might be right under the Geists'
noses. The hotel's unfinished wings jutted several hundred
feet out the back of the building in a straight line. The
section closest to the main lobby was almost finished, and
workers were busy there. The next three-story section was
walled and roofed, but no windows had been installed. The
last section looked like a wooden skeleton and still lacked
walls and a roof. Kate felt the second section was promising.

She sidled around the back, careful not to draw attention
to herself. When she'd moved out of the workers' vision, she
went up to where the windows would eventually be installed
and peeked in. The floors were bare plywood, the bathrooms had no fixtures yet, pipes and wiring were visible,
and electrical outlets had no cover plates. Open stairs led to
the second floor. If she and Chad could sneak in and make

their way upstairs, they'd be protected from the weather. More important, they couldn't be seen.

She started back to Chad, but then skidded to a stop outside the first section. Near the fountain, Mrs. Geist was talking to the same group of kids Kate had talked to earlier! Kate crouched behind a pile of dirt and bricks and watched. Kate guessed Mrs. Geist spoke Spanish, because they talked a long time and no one seemed to have trouble understanding.

When she was finished, Mrs. Geist looked around and then slipped the children a dollar each. They ran off laughing and squealing, while she hurried back into the hotel. It wouldn't be long, Kate knew, before Mrs. Geist found José, or he found her.

When Kate returned to the poorer part of town, Chad congratulated her on a good job and agreed they would need to check out the unfinished hotel section. Then Chad and Kate ran back to the river to see if the hair dye would work. Kate had only peeked in the sack to be sure it contained dye. She hadn't noticed anything else, and so she was as surprised as Chad when he pulled a tightly folded sheet of paper from the box.

"What's this?" he said.

"Probably the instructions," she said.

"No. It's from Eva, but it's written in Spanish."

Kate read over his shoulder: "Gnirif dauqs yadseut. Teg pleh kciuq. Eraweb. Stsieg kniht uoy evah kcapkcab htiw erup, tucnu nioreh htrow erom naht eno noillim nacirema srallod. Stsieg gnikool rof ti ta lla stsoc."

"What in the world is this?" Chad said.

"Let me see." Kate studied it for several minutes while Chad pulled out the hair dye.

"This isn't Spanish!" Kate said. "It's English!"

"That's English?" Chad said.

"Yes. C'mere and read each word backward."

They sat and read Eva Flores' message together. " 'Firing squad Tuesday. Get help quick.

Beware. Geists think you have backpack with pure, uncut heroin worth more than one million American dollars. Geists looking for it at all costs.' "

"We've got to bust Dad out of there!" Chad said. "I mean, I still want to try to call Uncle Bill, but we won't have time to wait for him. What are we supposed to do with this dye?"

"What do the directions say?"

"They're definitely in Spanish. And look, it's black dye."

"Oh, brother."

"Guess we can't be picky. I was hoping to use a little of it on my skin. But not even black people are *that* black."

Kate and Chad quickly mixed the dye and worked it through each other's hair. "Don't rinse," Kate said, "or it might all disappear."

But she needn't have worried about that. When they finished, their hair was so ridiculously jet black that they would have laughed their heads off at each other, had they not been in so much trouble.

"Your eyebrows are still blond," Chad said.

"So are yours."

So they each dipped a finger into the remaining dye and smeared it on the other's brows. Now they looked so ridiculous to each other that they couldn't help but giggle. Streaks of black ran down their foreheads, and their hands were stained black.

"Oh, now we'll really blend in," Chad said.

Kate wanted to laugh, but she wanted to cry too. Dad had till Tuesday, and the brown powder they hadn't recognized made their own lives worthless too. If it was worth as much as Eva said, the Geists wouldn't hesitate killing them to get it back.

"We've got to hide that heroin in case the Geists catch us," Kate said.

"We could bury it."

"As long as we can find it later," Kate said.

"I'd like to just dump it in the river. That way it will never hurt anyone."

"Me too, but wouldn't it harm the fish?"

"No, this river is so huge it would probably dilute the drug into a harmless level."

"Let's do it then," said Kate. "Otherwise, it's just a million dollars' worth of misery—if it were to be used by anyone."

"You're right! But let's just save out a little for evidence," suggested Chad. "And maybe a little more to tease the Geists."

"How would we do that?"

"I don't know yet, but the prison is so close to the hotel. We've got to get them away from there so we can get help for Dad. Let's keep trying to think of a plan." Chad took the big cellophane bag of brown powder and looked at Kate.

She shook her head. "I wonder if anyone has ever dumped a million dollars in a river before," she said.

"You want to do it?" he said.

"Go ahead," she said. "Just remember to save some for evidence."

Chad held the bag by one end and carefully shook it back and forth. The powder poured out and the slight breeze carried it out over the river and into the water. He saved a small amount of the powder in the cellophane bag.

"Let's hide that inside a sock," Kate said, pulling a pair from the leather bag.

Next they smeared their faces, hands, and feet with dust. Kate felt ridiculous as they walked toward town. She kept a careful eye out for Paco and the Geists as they neared the Branco Grande Prison.

"I'm gonna see what those kids are doing around the back," Chad said. "Whatever it is, the guards seem to leave them alone. Wait here."

Kate looked around at all the people sitting on the ground. Some were almost in the street, and others sat with their backs against the buildings across the street from the prison. Kate backed up against a wall and slid down, exhausted. With the sun directly overhead, she was sweating. She was also starving again. She watched from several feet away, hiding under her huge hat and baggy clothes. Her dirty, sandaled feet stuck out in front of her. She prayed for Chad and her dad. And she prayed they could get hold of Uncle Bill and that he would know what to do. She also came up with an idea of how to distract the Geists.

A few minutes later Chad returned and motioned for her to follow him back into an alley. "They're selling stuff to the inmates!" he said. "And they share the profits with the guards so they'll look the other way."

"What are they selling?"

"Well, you won't believe it, but it looks like hot potatoes. They go up to the window and call out, "Papas calientes! Papas calientes.""

Kate's stomach growled. Chad grinned. "Yeah, food sounds good to me too."

"Well, *we* can buy food, but Dad won't be able to buy anything. Don't those prisoners get fed?"

"Not enough, I guess. They really went for those potatoes."

"How do the prisoners pay for them?" Kate said. "Dad didn't have any money."

"Well, somebody's getting money in there, because the prisoners were handing money out through the bars."

"Where are those kids getting the potatoes?"

"From a vendor down the street."

"I'm gonna try it," Kate said. "We've got to know for sure if Dad's in there. If he is, I'm going to slip him some money and food." She took some local currency and the third wrist TV.

"Be careful!" Chad said.

Kate used two single bills of local currency and bought five roasted potatoes from the vender. She ate one of them, ignoring the slightly burned taste, saving one for Chad and planning to give the others to her dad. She moved around to the back of the prison and peeked in the first empty window she came to. The stench nearly knocked her over. No wonder! There were no bathrooms in there. It almost made her vomit. Not even any separate cells. And no beds. The floor was made of dirt. Hundreds of men milled around or lay around in clusters. They wore no uniforms. They were probably all wearing whatever they had on when they were sentenced and tossed in there.

Kate heard yelling and what she assumed was cursing in Spanish. A fight broke out at the far end, and most of the other prisoners drifted away from it, but then another broke out at the near end. Kate saw no sign of her dad. As kids crowded around the windows to watch, prisoners jostled for position to snatch a free potato or at least get the chance to buy one. Once they got one, they quickly stuffed it into their mouths.

Kate knifed her way closer and closer to a barred window opening. Finally she was close enough to see the huge, dark, open area. She looked and looked but no one even resembled her dad.

Finally she called, "Papas calientes," but she guessed she wasn't loud enough. The men in front of her ignored her and reached past her, buying potatoes and passing coins to the other kids.

"Spitfire!" Kate hollered, and a couple of men looked at her quizzically, then ignored her. She alternated between saying "papas calientes" and "Spitfire." Suddenly, from the edge of the crowd of prisoners pushed a lone figure. He shouldered his way past some and through others, causing them to grumble and threaten.

"Spitfire," Kate repeated as her father's haggard, unshaven face came into view. His eyes were desperate, as he reached through the bars and grabbed her wrist. She didn't want him to say her name. "I'm Conchita!" she whispered. "My brother Manny and I are selling potatoes. You want one?"

He nodded. He wore the same clothes he'd flown in, but he was barefoot, as were all the others. His shirttail hung out and his pants were torn.

"Have you eaten anything?"

Dad shook his head, and she handed him a potato with a wrist TV wrapped around it. No one else seemed to be listening, and if they were, they did not understand. Others were busy making their own transactions, buying food and cigarettes and who knew what else from the kids at the window.

"And here's your change, señor." Kate slipped Dad a handful of local currency. He stuffed the TV and the change into his pocket and quickly gorged on the potato.

"Stay out of sight, Conchita. Don't come here again. Call Uncle Bill. Go!"

"In a minute. I've got two more—"

But other kids elbowed her out of the way, and her dad disappeared. As much as Kate wanted to stay with her dad, she did what he said and took off running. A guard stopped her with a straight arm to the chest. "Señorita!" he said, sticking out his hand. Had he recognized her? What should she do? She didn't want to say anything. He rubbed his fingertips together as if he wanted money. She pulled out a single bill and handed it to him. He turned away, and Kate ran off to Chad.

"He's there!" she said, gasping. "Chad, he looks awful! I gave him a potato and a wrist TV and some money. It's terrible in there. No chairs, no bed, no plumbing, no light. They all just hang around on that dirt floor and try to get stuff from the kids on the street. He hadn't eaten."

"Then he needs more than one potato!"

"I know. I got shoved out of the way before I could give him the rest."

"Give me those!" Chad grabbed the potatoes and stood.

"Don't say your name," Kate said. "Go by Manny! Here, take him some more money. Take a bill for the guard too."

Kate hung back out of sight and watched Chad work his way to one of the windows. But then she was stunned to see a jeep skid to the curb. Paco was at the wheel. Most of the kids scattered, and the guards became quickly diligent.

Chad was one of the last to notice that he needed to get away from the barred opening.

"Manny!" Kate screamed when she saw the Geists' car pull in behind Paco.

Chad took off running, but away from Kate. He followed the other kids down the street and into an alley. Where would she ever catch up with him? She didn't want to follow right away because she would have to pass Paco and the Geists. Despite her dyed hair, disguise, and new bag, she didn't want to risk that.

Paco had leaped out of his jeep and was screaming at the guards. He handed a sheet of paper to one of them. Someone unlocked an entrance to the prison while one of the guards read from the sheet: "Arguello! Michaels! Sanchez!" He then rattled off a bunch of instructions Kate didn't understand.

She staggered from the prison, lugging the leather bag, when she heard Chad on her wrist TV. "Meet me at the hotel!" he said. "The kids were all saying, 'Busque, busque.' I think it means search."

"Oh, no," Kate said. "I hope Dad had time to get rid of the wrist TV." And she hoped those kids were right and that this was *only* a search.

The Plan

As Kate hurried through back streets toward the hotel, staticky noises came from her wrist TV. She ducked into an alley and set the bag down, then leaned against a building and tried to tune in whoever was on the other end.

A faint, jumpy image came from the liquid-crystal display, and she held it out into a stream of sunlight. Someone was messing with Dad's wrist TV, and it wasn't Dad! From what she could make out, it appeared someone was studying the wrist TV near a window in the prison. Occasionally she saw a face peer at the TV, as if he was trying to make it work. When he turned the TV over, Kate could see light, then a dark wall, the floor, bare feet, then his clothes. He wore no uniform! It wasn't a guard.

Had Dad lost the radio or given it to someone to hold for him? She saw the man reach toward the screen as he stared at it, pushing buttons. Suddenly the tinny sound returned, and she heard noises from within the prison. It sounded like the guards were yelling at the prisoners. She heard whacks and screams as if people were being beaten. She prayed it wasn't Dad.

It was clear the man on the other end of the wrist TV could see her now. He looked shocked and kept staring. Kate didn't feel like smiling, and she didn't know enough Spanish to tell him anything. "Hello," she said, praying the man wasn't standing near a guard who might hear her.

He raised his eyebrows and tried to repeat the greeting. "Alloo."

"Is my dad okay?" she said.

He frowned and shook the watch.

"Speak English, and stop shaking the watch!" Kate cried. "Is there an American there?"

"Alloo," the man said, grinning.

Kate wanted to burst into tears. "Adios," she said finally.

"Adios, poquita," he said.

She turned off the TV, telling herself to remember the word *poquita*.

Kate met Chad a block from the Plaza del Rio, and they agreed that he would go check out the nearly completed second wing to see if they'd be as well hidden as Kate thought. He ran off then to see if he could get in and out without being noticed.

"We can get in there without being seen," Chad said when he returned twenty minutes later.

"Good work. Let's go settle in." Kate followed her brother, and they covered the blocks in silence.

Before they got to the hotel, Kate used a little more of the local currency she had left to buy two small bouquets of flowers from a woman on the street. "I'll explain later," she told Chad.

Kate followed Chad around to the back of the hotel. He glanced over his shoulder before entering the half-finished wing. They found a room near the back from which they could watch the plaza and the fountain after dark. Kate let the heavy bag drop and sat on the floor. "This is going to be hard sleeping," she said, then added, "Chad, I have an idea. It's why I bought the flowers. I say we go to the desk with flower deliveries, one for the Geists and one for the Kennicotts. Only one of those names is registered here, right? I mean, they had to use one name or the other. We leave the flowers for them with notes and a little bit of the uncut heroin. We tell them where we'll meet them and when." She shrugged. "Maybe that will get them out of our hair for a while, and we can work on getting help for Dad."

"Great." Chad sat in silence. "Hey," he said finally, "when they tell us one of those names isn't registered in the hotel, we can take the leftover bouquet and have it delivered to

Eva Flores at the airport. Tell her where we are. See if she can call Uncle Bill."

"How would you get it to her?"

"I know. I'll ask the guy who drives the hotel shuttle back and forth to the airport. Bet he'd do it for American dollars."

Kate lay on her side and rested her head against the bag. His idea bothered her for some reason, but she couldn't put her finger on it. "I need to rest," she said, and she rolled onto her back and breathed heavily in the late afternoon heat.

Chad gently tugged the bag out from under her head, making her less comfortable. "Gotta find something to write with," he said. "These flowers won't last long in this heat."

Kate rolled suddenly to her side. "Chad, you know what we should have done with the heroin? We should have used it to buy Dad back."

"What do you mean? Give it to the guards?"

"No, that wouldn't be right. But we had a million dollar's worth of the Geists' stuff. And they're in this thing with General Valdez. We had the advantage."

Chad stared at her. "As far as they know, we still do. They don't know we threw it away."

Kate and Chad heard noises from their wrist TVs at the same time. They crawled over to the window opening, and Kate tried to tune in the transmission.

"Manny, Conchita," a voice spoke through the TV. It was Dad. "Do you read?"

The tiny screen was black.

"We're here," Kate said. "Go ahead."

Dad must have been hunched in a dark corner some-where, whispering into the radio. "What's happening?" he said. "Where are you?"

Kate told him, then, "Did you get searched?"

"Yeah, but not before I got a guy to hold the wrist TV for a while. I don't think he had any idea what it was."

"Did they beat you too?"

"I'm all right."

"But did they?"

"Don't worry about it. Just get help and get me out of here."

"We're trying!"

"Over and out," Dad said.

Kate wanted to keep him talking, but she didn't want to get him in trouble. Maybe someone had noticed him or was approaching. She would not try to make contact. They would just wait to hear from him. "Now what?"

"We do whatever we have to to get him out. What do you think of this?" Chad showed her the note he'd written to the Geists. It read, "We have what you want, and you have what we want. Ready to deal?" It was signed, *Your young "friends."*

"Good," she said.

"This should send them on a wild goose chase so we don't have to worry about them all the time," Chad said.

"But eventually we have to meet with them," Kate said. "If they think we have their million dollars' worth of drugs, we can use that to get them to talk Valdez into letting Dad go."

"I don't know, Kate. Sounds too risky."

"I know they have guns, but we've got guns too. They don't know we wouldn't use them."

He finally nodded. "Where should we tell them to meet us?"

"Somewhere out in the open so we can see if they bring soldiers with them. And where they can see only one of us, so they think the other one has their drugs. We have to convince them that if one of us doesn't get back to the other one safely, they'll never get their drugs."

"Wow, Kate, how do you think of all this stuff?"

"I don't know," she said. "Women's intuition, I guess."

Chad shook his head. "I can't see Valdez just giving Dad the plane back, giving him fuel, and letting him leave the country. Somehow we've got to get Uncle Bill to let the U.S. government know what's going on."

Kate and Chad settled on two locations for their meetings, one with the Geists, one with Eva Flores. They would tell the Geists to meet them at the bend in the river, near where they had dumped the drugs. The Geists would be instructed to come together but to bring no one else. They'd have to park at least a quarter mile away and walk to the spot, so Kate and Chad could see if they brought anyone with them.

Kate and Chad would also give Eva Flores the names of two cross streets in town, along with directions to a back alley. The note to Eva asked that she meet them at sundown. He put Eva's note with her flowers. They would meet the Geists an hour after talking to Eva. And they would stick together. While Chad negotiated with the Geists, Kate would be up a tree behind him.

Chad added the meeting location to the Geists' note. Then he sprinkled a small amount of the leftover heroin into the envelope and placed it in with their flowers. Chad headed down to the front desk, and Kate listened by wrist TV.

"English?" he said to the girl.

"Sí. I mean, yes!"

"Flower deliveries for two guests. Geist and Kennicott."

There was a long pause, then, "I'm sorry, *poquito*, but there is no one here under the name Geist. Are they at another hotel?"

"Maybe," Chad said. "I'll check."

"Kennicott is in room 514. You want to deliver them yourself?"

"Are they here?" Chad said. Kate knew that was unlikely. They had just seen the Geists at the prison.

"Let me ring their room and see," she said. "Oh! Their car just pulled up! Wait here and you'll get a tip."

"No, I've got to get going," Chad said. "More deliveries."

Kate heard him run away. She knew he wouldn't risk coming back to where she was for a while—it was too close to the Geists. She crawled to the window opening and peeked out. There was Chad, running as fast as he could with a bouquet of flowers in his hand. Soon Mr. Geist appeared, but he wasn't running. He scanned the area and then turned back into the hotel.

"You're not being followed, Manny," Kate transmitted. "But you'd better stay out of sight for a while."

"That was close. Can you see their car?"

Kate craned her neck. "Yes. It's in the side lot near the front."

"Let me know if they leave so I can get Eva's flowers and note to the shuttle guy. And I'll try to find us some food."

"Good, I'm starving." Forty minutes later, Kate let Chad know the Geists were on the move. Not long after that he sneaked back up to their perch.

"Worked perfectly," he said. "The guy was thrilled."

"But will he do it?"

"Why not? He even said he knew who Eva Flores was and would deliver the bouquet himself." Chad unrolled the edge of his baggy shirt to reveal the food he'd bought.

"What's that?" Kate said, smelling cooked meat and onions.

"*Flautas*, I think they call them. Meat wrapped in tortillas."

Kate wolfed down two. Spicy or not, they tasted great. "Should we tell Dad what we're up to?" she said.

"No! If we call him at the wrong time, someone might hear the wrist TV and he'd be in trouble. We have to wait to hear from him."

Kate and Chad sat on the floor, resting, sweating, and discussing what Chad would say to the Geists if they showed up an hour after sundown.

"By then," Kate said, "Eva should have had time to make a phone call. Do you know Uncle Bill's number?"

"No, but Dad's address and phone book is in the bag with his wallet." He dug it out and found the number.

"Let me see that wallet again," Kate said. She picked through it for a minute, then proudly held up a plastic card. "Bingo!"

"Dad's phone card!" Chad said. "Perfect! Eva should be able to use this to call the States from just about any phone. And it won't show up on a phone record no matter where she calls from."

"Yeah," Kate said, "but remember where we are."

"It has to work," Chad said. "I just know if she can get through to Uncle Bill, he'll know who to contact and we'll get some action."

Their wrist TVs crackled then. "Spitfire?" Dad whispered.

"Spitfire here, go ahead."

"Guys in here tell me executions take place a minute after midnight. Next one is scheduled for twelve-oh-one Tuesday. That's a minute after midnight tomorrow night. And I think I'm the target."

"They'll have to kill *us* first," Kate said. "If we can't get help by then, we'll come down there with these guns."

"No! Don't do anything stupid. Now—"

"We'll do whatever we have to do," Kate said. "And I mean it!"

But Dad's TV had fallen silent.

Dark couldn't come soon enough for Kate. The day was hotter than the one before, and besides, she had never been one for sitting around and doing nothing. She had no idea where the Geists were or what they were up to. General Valdez was apparently determined to have Dad put to death with no trial and little time to reconsider. Paco seemed to be all over town trying to find the "escapees" and make up for his mistake of finding the stuff he wasn't supposed to find.

Occasionally Kate or Chad would peek out the window to see whether the Geists' car was there or not. They could do little else until it began to grow dark. If the Geists' car was at the hotel when Kate and Chad left, they would walk in a different direction so they wouldn't be noticed so easily. But if the car was not there, it could be anywhere, and they would have to be on the lookout for the Geists all the time.

When the sun finally began to dip below the horizon, Kate and Chad grabbed the bag, checked the window, and headed out. The Geists' car was back in place, and Kate and Chad left the hotel through the back way. They circled around the side streets to get to the location where they hoped to meet Eva Flores.

Kate kept peeking behind her as they hurried through the city. As far as she could tell, no one was following them. But when they were within a couple of blocks of the pre-arranged spot, Chad suddenly stopped. Kate wasn't looking and bumped into him. He immediately shushed her.

"What?" she said.

He pointed. There, parked on the side of the street, was a military jeep identical to the ones at the airport. Kate and Chad quickly ducked into an alley and circled around to where they could see the jeep from the front. The headlight was broken and the bumper creased. Kate and Chad stared at each other. They were still two blocks from where they were supposed to meet Eva.

They went the long way around, keeping on the alert for soldiers all the way. But they saw none. Kate couldn't imagine why anyone from the airport would be in that area unless they had followed Eva or knew where she was going. Chad walked Kate to the opposite end of the alley where they were supposed to meet Eva.

There, ramrod straight as a statue, stood a soldier in a camouflage uniform.

The Meetings

"Wait!" Chad whispered. "Back up. I don't think he's seen us."

"We're dead," Kate said. "I'll bet they have us surrounded."

"He doesn't know it's us yet," Chad said. "We'd better make a run for it before that guy spots us and tells his friends we're here."

"Back to the hotel?"

"Anywhere. We can't just walk into a trap. Should we split up?"

"Maybe. You want to take one of the guns?"

"What are you, crazy? What're we gonna do, go blast Dad out of prison?"

"We might as well try, Chad. I'm telling you, I've got a feeling we're surrounded."

"All right, let's go. If we get away, I'll meet you at the river in an hour."

And with that they took off running. But before she had gone twenty feet, Kate heard someone call, "Conchita! Manny! It's me!"

Kate skidded to a stop and whirled. In full camouflage, her hair tucked up under a helmet, Eva Flores waited for them near the alley to their right. They ran to her.

"Hello, kids," she said. "I brought these extra clothes and changed after I was away from the airport. I often drive to town on errands." She looked up and down the alley in both directions. "I'm sorry we have to meet here, but you can't be seen with me. People are all over the place looking for you. The Kennicotts are at the Plaza del Rio."

"We know," Kate and Chad said in unison.

"You were spotted at a barn on the edge of town."

"We know."

"Paco says someone even thought he saw you at the prison. Your father was searched and beaten. I'm sorry to tell you—he is to die just after midnight tomorrow night."

"No!" Kate cried. "Eva, we have to get him out of there. Can you call the United States for us?"

"Maybe. It is very dangerous."

"You can make the call with my dad's phone credit card," Chad said.

"Still, it puts me in grave danger," Eva said. "Maybe you can do something for me in exchange."

"What can we do?"

"Can you get me asylum?"

"Asylum? What's that?"

"Refuge. Sanctuary."

Kate and Chad looked at each other, confused. Kate had heard those words but wasn't sure what they meant.

"How do we do that?"

"It's simple," Eva said. "If we can somehow get your father out of this mess, you help me get back to my home country."

"Which is?"

"Ecuador. I met Valdez in military training there and worked for him all the way up to when he became a rebel and began opposing established military regimes. But now it has gone too far and I see him for who he is. I want to return to my family, but I need a way out."

"We have to trust you," Kate said. "We hardly know you, but we know you risked your life to help us escape. And if you can do anything to help us get our dad out of prison, we promise you he will get you to Ecuador."

Eva knelt in the alley. "Then I will risk everything," she whispered. "Tell me what to do and I will do it."

Kate and Chad gave her their dad's phone card and the number for their Uncle Bill in Portland. "Tell him everything that's going on. He'll know what to do."

"What will he do?" Eva said.

"He'll get the United States government and even the military involved, if he has to."

"I'll do it," Eva said. "Even if I have to risk doing it from a phone at the airport, I will do this. But I must not be revealed as one who has helped you until it is clear I can go with you and not be in danger. As corrupt and criminal as Valdez is, he will accuse me of an act of treason punishable by death. I should have turned him in to President Guillen months ago. Our president is an honorable man, but he does not know everything about Valdez."

Kate and Chad nodded. "I just know this is going to work," Kate said. "Dad will be free. We will be free. And you will be free."

"I'd better go," Eva said.

"Meet us back here in two hours," Chad said. "And Eva, if we're not here, do whatever you have to do to get our dad free, and tell him we promised he would take you to Ecuador."

Kate and Chad then headed toward the river. "Maybe we should just forget about the Geists," Kate said as they ran. "Let them show up and wonder where we are."

"No," Chad said. "We should go through with the plan. Make them ask Valdez to release Dad so they can get their million dollars' worth of dope back."

"But what if he says we have to turn over the drugs or he'll execute Dad?"

Chad just shook his head. "All I know," he said, "is that we need to buy some time in case it takes a while for Uncle Bill to get hold of somebody who can do something. Don't forget this is Sunday."

Kate shuddered. "And let's not forget we've got only a little more than twenty-four hours to work with."

They arrived at the river half an hour before they were supposed to meet the Geists. Chad helped Kate lug the leather bag up a tree about forty feet behind the spot he'd told them to meet him. "Just watch and listen," he said, moving away.

Kate and Chad whispered to each other over their wrist TVs while they waited for the Geists. "Let's not do anything stupid," Chad said.

"What if they grab you and force you to tell them where their drugs are?"

"They won't. They know that if they want their drugs back, they have to deal with me."

"I wish I knew how to use these guns," Kate said.

"Well, you don't, so don't even think about it. They're not loaded, and I wouldn't know how to do it."

"These are just clips," Kate said. "All you do is snap them in."

"Well, don't."

"Don't worry."

It was pitch black when Kate and Chad noticed headlights turning off the main road, onto the dirt road, and then down a narrow path toward the river. A couple of hundred feet from Chad, where the ground became rough and uneven, the car stopped. Kate could hardly hear from that distance, but it sounded as if the Geists had left it running. The lights were still on, and the car was parked facing the river, maybe ten feet from the bank, which was steep at that point.

Though the headlights pointed more toward the river than toward Chad, Kate could make out two figures headed toward them. They slowly came closer, and when they were within about a hundred feet, Chad shouted, "Are you alone?"

"We're alone, you little dirt ball," Mr. Geist called. "Are you?"

"Yeah, I'd be stupid enough to meet you two alone out here in the dark in the middle of nowhere."

"Well, you're pretty stupid to think you can walk off with something of ours."

"Oh, that was yours? It was in my sister's backpack."

When the Geists were about twenty feet from Chad, he told them to stop.

"How about you just give us back our stuff and we promise you won't die when your dad does?"

"Sounds like you don't really want your stuff back," Chad said.

"Just tell us where it is."

Chad's voice sounded more confident than he was, Kate knew. "Oh, sure, that would be smart. Here's the deal. We'll give you back your guns and ammunition and the rest of the drugs when my dad's plane is fueled up, cleared for takeoff, and we're all allowed back on it. Dad will even pay for the fuel."

"Why don't we just take you and make your sister buy you back with what belongs to us?"

"You could never catch me," Chad said.

"How do you know we don't have you surrounded?"

"How do you know we didn't already flush your dope down the river?"

"You wouldn't be that stupid," Mr. Geist said. "You know it's your only hope of getting your dad out of prison."

Kate had heard enough. She dug into the bag and pulled out a Luger. She knew it was empty, but it felt heavy and ugly and cold in her hand. "How do you know I don't have your own gun pointed right at your head?" she hollered.

The Geists looked up quickly, but Kate knew they couldn't see her in the tree.

"Listen," Mrs. Geist spoke for the first time, "we know you have no reason to believe or trust us. But we're here unarmed. You don't need to shoot us."

Kate alternated pointing the gun at Mr. Geist and then Mrs. Geist. What would it be like to pull the trigger? She put her index finger on it, but of course, the empty gun would make only a metallic snapping sound, and then they would know she was sitting up there with an unloaded weapon. Suddenly an idea hit her. She put the weapon back in the bag and quietly climbed out of the tree. It was totally dark other than the light from the car's headlamps. She circled far outside the Geists' and her brother's fields of vision, heading for their car.

She wanted to know whether it was running and if anyone else was around. She listened on her wrist TV as Mrs. Geist talked on. "We have no influence over what happened to your father. It was not what we intended. We thought you would stay a few days and fly home none the wiser. Something went wrong. It wasn't *our* fault. We didn't want to see your father go to prison. We know he is innocent. We just used him."

"You think I don't know that you're in this deal with General Valdez?" Chad said. "You tell him to let our dad go. That's the only way you'll see your stuff again."

Everything was silent for a moment. "How do we know you'll keep up your end of the bargain?" Mr. Geist finally asked.

"Why wouldn't we? All we want is our dad back."

Kate reached the Geists' car, which was still running. No one else was around. She tiptoed up and peered in the window of the back door. There on the seat lay two high-powered weapons.

Kate was suddenly overcome with bitterness toward this couple. She didn't know what their real names were. She didn't know their history, what they were up to, or why they had lied to get her father to fly them to Amazonia. All she knew was that they had treated her so nice in Boise that she had put away all her doubts and misgivings about them.

She was mad at herself, angry at them, and scared they would try to do something to Chad or to her just to get their precious drugs back. What were these weapons all about? Did the Geists plan to come back and shoot them? Kate didn't know, but she knew she had to do something.

She could holler at Chad that the Geists had weapons in the car. She could throw the weapons in the river. Why had they left the engine running? Were they planning a quick getaway?

Kate impulsively opened the driver's-side door and grabbed the gearshift. She tried to shift the car into drive, but it wouldn't budge. Then she remembered that on her dad's car, he had to push on the brake pedal to shift into drive. One foot still on the ground, she stepped into the car and placed her right foot on the brake pedal. But standing awkwardly like that didn't give her enough leverage.

Oglesby Union Church

Oglesby, Illinois

She slipped into the car and sat behind the wheel. She looked back at Chad and the Geists. She could hear them talking on her wrist TV, but she couldn't see them. "Why don't you let us drive you out to the airport and we'll talk this over with the general?" Mrs. Geist was saying.

"You must think kids are stupid," Chad said. "No deal. You get my dad out of that prison and out to the airport and then we'll come there."

"I'll tell you what I'm going to do, you little slime," Mr. Geist said. "I'm gonna break your neck and see if your little sister has the guts to shoot me. What do you think of that?"

Kate sat in the car with her left foot still on the ground. She pushed on the brake pedal and shifted into drive. She felt the gears engage. All she had to do was let her foot off the brake and the car would head toward the river, just a few feet away.

On her wrist she heard Chad's less than confident voice. "If you hurt me, my sister might shoot you. But even if she doesn't, you'll never get your stuff back."

"I'm through messing with you," Mr. Geist said.

"Don't do it," Mrs. Geist said.

Kate let up on the brake and jumped out of the car. It began rolling slowly, crunching the dry ground. When the front wheels of the all-wheel-drive car dropped over the edge of the river bank, the wheels continued to turn, but they gripped only air. The car's headlights now pointed into the water, and the under-carriage of the car had become hung up. The car teetered on the edge of the bank.

It rocked there, and every time the back tires touched the ground they moved the car forward another few inches before it rocked some more, pulling the back tires off the ground. Kate ran straight back about a hundred feet. She could hear the Geists swearing and knew they were running toward the car.

She stood still in the darkness as they approached. "What the devil!" Mr. Geist shouted. "Did you leave it in drive?"

"I wasn't driving, you idiot," his wife said. "You were."

"Well, I didn't leave it in gear!"

"Get the rifles," Mrs. Geist said.

"I've got to get the stuff from the trunk first! Do you realize what we have in there? We can replace the weapons, but we're talking over ten million bucks in the trunk!"

"Be careful," she said.

"Shut up! Where are the keys?"

"In the ignition, stupid."

"Can't I pop the trunk from a switch in the glove box?" he said.

"I don't know! This is a rental car. Just do what you have to do!"

"You're a big help."

"You're the one who didn't want to risk leaving the stuff in the hotel!" she snapped. " 'Nobody will find it in the trunk,' you said."

"Just get out of my way," he said.

Mr. Geist hurried to the other side of the car and carefully opened the front passenger door. He pushed the button on the glove compartment, which made the car teeter a little farther forward.

"Careful!" Mrs. Geist hollered.

"Shut up!" he shouted.

He pushed another button and the trunk flew open, shifting the weight of the car and making it rock enough so that the rear wheels grabbed the ground solidly one more time. Mrs. Geist rushed toward the open trunk as Mr. Geist jumped away from the moving car.

With great squeaking and scraping and crunching, the car plunged straight down into the river. The gigantic splash drenched both the Geists.

"No! No! No!" Mr. Geist yelled as he tore at his hair and jumped up and down.

The car must have flipped over, Kate decided, because the bobbing headlights now faced the bank. With a gurgle and bubbles, the car began to sink.

Kate raced back to the tree to get the leather bag, hoping Chad was still there and was all right.

The Rescue

Kate found Chad calling for her from the tree she'd hidden in. "I'm right here," she said.

He scrambled down. "Where have you been? Mr. Geist was trying to kill me."

"Who do you think put their car on the edge of the river bank?"

"You? Why?"

"It got their attention away from you, didn't it?"

"For a while. We've got to get out of here."

Kate and Chad stared into the distance where the car lights were quickly disappearing under the water. They heard a splash, then Mrs. Geist telling her husband to be careful, and him telling her to shut up again. He must have jumped into the water to salvage whatever he could.

"There were high-powered weapons in there," Kate said, as they ran off into the darkness, farther and farther from town. "You think they'll come after us?"

"Not without light. We'd better be careful not to get lost. We've got to get back to Eva soon."

"Let's wait here then," Kate said, "and see if we hear anything. Then we can circle around and get back to town."

Kate and Chad sat panting near a grove of trees, and Kate pulled out the gun she had pointed at the Geists. "Can you see this?" she said.

"No, what?"

"The Luger."

"You made them think you were actually pointing it at them."

"I was! It's not loaded, Chad. You told me that yourself."

"You know Dad says there's no such thing as an unloaded gun."

"Yeah, but I wasn't going to pull the trigger. You think I wanted them to know it wasn't loaded?" She pointed the gun into the air. "It would have made a sound like this." And she pulled the trigger.

The boom was so deafening that both kids hit the ground. Kate's right ear rang, but she could hear enough out of her left.

"I can't believe you did that!" Chad said. "You were pointing that gun at the Geists for real?"

"Yes," she said, feeling sobs invade her throat. "And I had my finger on the trigger, too!"

"Kate!"

"Chad! The clip isn't even in it! Feel!"

She handed him the Luger. "You're right!" he said. "Maybe it's a trick gun or something. Whatever it is, don't touch it again."

"You think the Geists heard that?"

"They had to."

"Then let's get out of here."

Kate was shaky. What if she had shot someone? It didn't matter if it was the Geists, Chad, or herself, she would never have gotten over it. She felt so stupid! "I'm sorry, Chad. That was really dumb."

"It sure proves Dad's point about guns, doesn't it?" He laughed.

"What's funny?"

"I was just thinking ... if you had shot the gun into the air when you were in the tree, the Geists would have fainted."

"So would I," Kate said.

Half an hour later they arrived at the edge of town. They stopped when they heard a crackly noise from their wrist TVs. "Spitfire?"

"Dad! Can you hear us?"

"I heard all of that! I didn't want to call until I was sure you were alone. What in the world were you doing, meeting with the Geists? Don't you realize how dangerous they must be? I mean I appreciate it, but you've got to get to Uncle Bill."

"We're trying," Chad said. "But they left drugs in Kate's backpack and we found out it was worth a million dollars."

"Just get rid of it and get help," Dad said. "These people will stop at nothing. How did Kate get her backpack anyway?"

"I'll tell you later," Kate said. "You probably know it was the young woman at the tribunal who helped us escape."

"I wondered. I heard you overpowered her, but she didn't seem hurt. It didn't add up to me, and it probably won't add up to anyone else either. You're all in danger."

"She's helping us," Chad said, "and we need her, Dad."

"Quiet!" Dad said. "Someone's—"

His TV transmission cut out, and they didn't dare risk transmitting to him until they heard from him. Kate worried the Geists had already gotten to Valdez and he had sent someone to the prison to beat him again—or worse—for what she and Chad did.

They ran to where they had agreed to meet Eva. She was there, sitting in the darkness.

"Eva!" Kate hurried to her side. "Did you reach our uncle?"

"I did," she said, "and I did not have to risk using an airport phone. I remembered a distant relative on the outskirts of town who has a phone. It took half an hour to get a line out of the country, but I did talk to your Uncle Bill. He did not trust me and insisted on talking to one of you."

"We'll talk to him, but when and where?"

"Get into the jeep and stay down out of sight. I will take you to the phone. I also reached President Guillen and told him everything. I think he believes me. He wants to keep the United States out of this at all costs. For one thing, he is afraid Valdez might attack, pretending it is self-defense, if Americans land at the airport. The president wants to solve this himself. He wants me to call him back to finalize a plan."

"Do you trust him?" Chad said.

"I have to. I have no choice anymore."

Kate and Chad lay down on the floor of the back seat of the jeep, and Eva roared to the outskirts of town. "Do you believe her?" Chad whispered. "Or do you think she has already been caught and is taking us somewhere for Valdez?"

"No way," Kate said. "Eva is with us. She would not betray us."

"How can you be so sure?"

"Women's intuition," Kate said.

Soon the jeep braked behind a small house in a remote area. Someone peeked out the window, and Kate and Chad jumped down and followed Eva inside. Her relatives, a shy couple with a bunch of children, herded all the kids into another room and left Eva, Kate, and Chad alone with the phone.

Eva got connected with the international operator in Spanish. She read off the card numbers, while Kate and Chad waited impatiently beside her. "Let me talk to him," Kate whispered to Chad.

"That's fine," he said. "Just be quick and tell him everything."

Eva hung up. "The operator will call me back when she's made the connection." She went into the other room to talk with her relatives, then brought them all out to meet Kate and Chad. None spoke English, so Eva translated.

The phone rang and Eva answered. "Yes, sir, your niece is right here."

"Uncle Bill?"

"Kate, honey, are you all right?"

"Yes, Uncle Bill. Let me tell you—"

"Before you say anything, let me ask you some questions. Is anyone else on the line?"

"No."

"Are you sure?"

"Pretty sure."

"Is the woman who called me really Mrs. Geist?"

"No!"

"You're sure?"

"Totally."

"Is she really a friend who helped you escape?"

"Yes, Uncle Bill. Everything she told you is true."

"And you're not just saying this because you're being threatened?"

"No!"

"Praise the Lord!" he said. "Listen, Kate. The U.S. government knows all about the Geists. Someone called here looking to get hold of your dad not too long after you guys took off from Boise. They wanted to warn him about the Geists, that they were phonies and drug runners. They were taking some of their uncut stuff down there to show the Amazonians how they processed heroin and cocaine. U.S. agents had been tracking them for months, but our government didn't learn of their trip until the last minute."

"So what did you do?" Kate said.

"Just in case the woman who called me was telling the truth, I told the military and our government everything. They've had planes in Chile and Argentina since yesterday anyway, knowing the Geists are down there, and they're ready to make an air strike if necessary. The state department is prepared to insist that it will not recognize Amazonia as an independent country until your dad has been released."

"You'd better talk to Eva about that," Kate said. "She thinks the president of Amazonia will help us."

"Would he turn over the Geists to the U.S. government?"

"Talk to her, Uncle Bill."

"Honey?"

"Yes."

"Is Chad there?"

"Sure. You want to talk to him?"

"Better not take the time right now. Just tell him we love you guys, and we're praying for you, and we will get you all out of there safely."

Kate handed the phone to Eva and began to feel optimistic for the first time since the family had landed in South America.

Eva listened a moment, then said, "Sir, let me talk to our president about that. I do not believe there will be any reason to bring warplanes in. Let me give President Guillen your ideas and get him in touch with your government and military. Thank you, sir."

"Let me talk to him," Chad said.

Eva looked troubled, like she did not want to take any more time. But she handed Chad the phone.

"One more thing, Uncle Bill," he said. "We promised Eva she could get back to Ecuador if she helped us."

Eva spent the next hour on the phone connected to the president's vacation home a hundred miles away. They seemed to be concocting an elaborate scheme. When she hung up, she smiled at Kate and Chad. "I might not have to go back to Ecuador after all. I might want to stay here and continue working for the president. He is a good man. He is going to do the right thing. He says if you have evidence, he will make Valdez pay."

Eva told them the plan on the way back to the meeting place, where they would split up. "Lay low tonight," she said, "and I will arrange for you to be captured here tomorrow morning, probably by Paco."

Kate jerked. "What! Why?"

"You will not be in danger. The president will tell Valdez that he is coming to the airport to meet and honor the American couple who helped expose an arms and drug smuggler. He will also say that he wants the prisoner there to be publicly humiliated by the ceremony." She turned a corner. "I will tell Valdez that you called the airport and have said you would surrender if it might help your father's cause in any way. That way he can have your father and his children there as a surprise for the president." Eva turned down the alley. "The Geists will be there, of course, for their honor. At the proper time, the tables will be turned."

Before leaving, they turned the guns, ammunition, and remaining dope in Kate's sock over to Eva. "Do you know anything about weapons?" Kate asked their new friend.

"Sure."

"Why would a Luger like this fire when there is no clip in it?"

"Because one shell remains in the chamber when a clip is removed. You always have to be careful and check that."

"No kidding," Kate said.

The kids sneaked into their uncomfortable, unfinished hotel room that night but found sleep impossible. In the morning they heard a commotion and peeked outside to see the well-dressed Geists proudly climbing into an airport military jeep. The excitement of what the day would bring was almost unbearable to Kate.

Once the Geists were gone, she and Chad packed their leather bag and ran to the meeting place. Two jeeps waited, loaded with soldiers. Kate was terrified that these military men might take justice into their own hands and kill them, just for the honor of it. She shook when Paco leveled his weapon at them and ordered them into a jeep.

"Good to surrender," he said, as his driver roared off. "Right thing to do. Can't help father, but now live in state orphanage."

Neither Kate nor Chad responded.

When they arrived at the airport it seemed every soldier wore a clean, pressed uniform. Many worked around the grounds, sprucing up the place for the president's visit. They saw a review platform being hastily built near the runway. When Kate and Chad were ushered inside, General Valdez and his tribunal, including Eva Flores, were waiting for them in the interrogation room. The Geists were not in sight, but soon after Kate and Chad were seated, Valdez asked the guards to bring in their father.

It broke Kate's heart to see how terrible he looked. His face was bruised and scraped, and one eye was swollen. He limped, still barefoot. He had not shaved, and his clothes were filthy. But he communicated to Kate and Chad with his eyes. It was clear he had no idea what this was all about, and Kate wanted with everything in her to tell him it was almost over, and he would soon be free.

General Valdez, in his dress uniform, looked delighted. "Here we all are again," he announced. "And *el presidente* is on his way."

Dad looked surprised, but he said nothing.

"The prisoner is not so talkative today, eh?" Valdez said.

"No, sir," Dad said. "I beg your mercy on my children."

Kate didn't want to see him beg, but she knew he believed it was his last hope for them.

"Send them back to the United States to be with people who love them," Dad added.

"Silence!" Valdez said. He turned to the others. "Allow me to be alone with the prisoners."

The older woman, the other two officers, and Eva Flores gathered up their papers and notebooks. Eva stacked her tape recorder and her papers on a table near the wall, then followed the rest of the officers and several soldiers into the hall.

Soon the AirQuest Aventures team was alone in the room with General Valdez. "Your children are going nowhere, señor," he said. "As I told you before, they will be guests of one of our fine orphanages."

"Don't do this," Dad said.

Now Valdez was angry. He stood. "This will be a great day. The *presidente* will honor me and the Kennicotts in front of your face. You proclaim your ignorance, and yet you stole what the Kennicotts brought me."

"I didn't steal—"

"Your children, señor! Your children! What would they be doing with a million dollars' worth of contraband? Even if you did nothing, you should die for their theft."

"We didn't steal anything," Kate said. "Your friends put it into my backpack. I didn't even know I had it."

"But now you know, and you know it is mine. And I want to know where the rest of it is."

"I dumped it in the river," Chad said.

Valdez appeared ready to explode. "I do not believe that," he said. "You will tell me when you see your father tortured to within an inch of his life."

Valdez called for guards to take the family to a waiting area. They were not allowed to speak. Kate was bursting, wanting to wink at her dad, to smile, to tell him everything. But she could not. Soon they heard a plane landing, and the family was led out into the sun for the ceremony.

President Guillen was a small man with a thin mustache and vivid, dark eyes. He was not dressed in a uniform but wore a suit. The Amazonian airport military stood proudly in a line as Valdez introduced the president and his entourage of personal bodyguards. They saluted smartly, and he walked down the row inspecting them.

The president placed his hands on each officer's shoulders and leaned close for a personal greeting. Kate noticed that Eva spoke briefly with him and then slipped him a small package.

The Kennicotts waited proudly on chairs on the platform, where they were joined by Valdez, Guillen, and the tribunal, including Eva Flores. The Michaels family waited off to the side, guarded by two soldiers.

General Valdez took the microphone. "We are proud to welcome our leader, the honorable President Manuel Guillen. He has come to honor our efforts in apprehending an American smuggler and to also honor those Americans who aided in the arrest. President Guillen."

Guillen thanked the general and began. "First, I would ask that the soldiers guarding the prisoners be replaced by two of my own men, so that they may join the rest of the airport military."

The soldiers looked at Valdez, who nodded.

Guillen spoke directly to the guards. "You may leave your weapons there."

Again the guards looked to Valdez, and again he nodded.

"And General Valdez, I would like to have your troops leave their weapons where they stand and move directly in front of me."

"I don't understand," Valdez said, standing.

"It will become clear to you, General, if you please."

Valdez gestured to his troops, and they left their weapons on the ground and paraded in front of the podium to stand in front of President Guillen.

"And now I would ask that my men arrest the airport troops, including General Valdez and his officers, and the American couple on the platform."

Valdez stood, flush-faced and sputtering. "But, sir, I—"

"General, I know what has gone on here, and it will not be tolerated. The sovereign state of Amazonia will be run by men and women who cherish the law and freedom."

"But, sir, I—"

"Or perhaps you would prefer that I play a tape of the conversation you just had with your prisoners, in which you admit that the smuggled goods belonged to you." Valdez fell silent and was handcuffed. "We will determine later how many of your troops should be tried along with you, Señor Valdez."

Dad stood there with his eyes wide and his mouth open, and Kate began to jabber at him. In a little more than a minute she gushed the whole story, right up to nearly shooting the Geists, setting up their car to drop into the river, and talking to Uncle Bill on the phone.

"A United States military plane will land here in a few minutes," President Guillen said. "It will extradite the Geists for trial in their own country and make sure the Michaels family is healthy before they return home as well."

"I want to go home now," Dad whispered.

"But you can't," Kate said. "You need someone to look at your wounds, and you need at least two days of rest."

Dad looked at her and shook his head. "I'd rather rest at home."

"You can rest there too, but you need at least two days before you fly a plane again."

"What do you think, Chad?" Dad said.

Chad shrugged. "Don't look at me."

Kate grinned. "Dad," she said, "I don't think Chad will ever argue against women's intuition again."

AirQuestAdventures

DiSaSTeR
in the Yukon

zonderkidz

#1 BEST-SELLING AUTHOR
JERRY B. JENKINS

Kate's Friend

It wasn't the news Chad Michaels wanted to hear.

"Suzie Q and her family are moving to the Yukon!" his sister Kate exulted one night at the dinner table.

Of course Kate would be thrilled. She and Susan Quenton had been playmates the first six years of their lives, back in Oklahoma. But that was five years ago, and all Chad remembered was Suzie Q as a spoiled brat.

"No kidding?" Dad said. "I told her dad Old Sparrow Christian Boarding School was looking for a president, but I had no idea he'd actually go for it, the school being so far into Yukon Territory."

"How far?" Kate said, her mouth full. "Will I get to see her a lot?"

Dad squinted. "Old Sparrow is near the Canadian border, at least two hundred miles east." He smiled. "I can't imagine Suzie Q in that environment, can you? I mean, those mountains, the river frozen most of the year, and snow, snow, and more snow."

"We all love that, Dad," Kate said. "Why shouldn't they?"

"Oh, *they* will," Chad said. "It's that spoiled only child who's in for a surprise."

"Chad!" Kate said, slamming her fork on the table. "You don't know Suzie anymore. She's not still six, you know."

"Come on, Kate. I'll bet she's still a dumb little kid."

"Now Chad," Dad said, "Kate's kept up with Suzie by email all these years, and—"

"And she's sweet," Kate said. "And wonderful."

"I'll believe it when I see it," Chad said, looking away from Kate's withering stare.

"How's she doing with her—what is it—diabetes?"

"Yeah," Kate said. "She gives herself shots every day. She says her mom is shipping a six-month supply of insulin up here before the heavy snow season."

"The heavy snow season is already here," Dad said. "Hope she knows that. When do they arrive?"

"They'll be at the school by the end of the week," Kate said.

Dad raised his eyebrows. "Something different for Hugh; he's been an Air Force chaplain for so long. But he'll do fine. I do wonder how Margie will do in this climate."

"Let alone Suzie Q," Chad said, shaking his head.

"Leave her alone," Kate said. "You've never given her a chance."

Chad smirked. "Maybe she'll grow up one of these days."

"She's already grown up, Chad," Kate said. "You're just too critical. How would you like to have to give yourself shots every day?"

"I'm not saying I don't feel sorry for her. But why does she have to be such a—"

"You have no idea what kind of a person she is now," Kate said. "Just be glad you're not judged by how you acted five years ago."

Well, that was true, but Chad wasn't about to admit it.

Dad stood and signaled the kids to help clear the table. "Kate," he said, "have Suzie Q tell her parents that I'll email them. We have to get you two together soon."

"When, Dad?"

"Soon. If we wait even until November, it'll be too hard to drive that close to Canada. Wouldn't surprise me if the Porcupine River is already frozen and snowed over."

That night before going to bed, Chad spent some time online keeping up with his sports statistics from the lower forty-eight states. Then he checked the saved email files to see what Kate and Dad had written to the Quentons. Kate had written, "Chad doesn't say so, but I think he's as excited about seeing you again as I am."

Could she really think that? No way. It wasn't like Kate to lie. Maybe she just wanted Susie Q to feel welcome in the Yukon or something. Or maybe Kate thought he was hiding some secret interest in Suzie Q. If she believed that, she couldn't be more wrong.

Kate also told Suzie Q about the wrist radios she had converted into wrist TVs. "They work for only about a mile, and the picture's fuzzy. We can't watch each other on our wrists from two hundred miles away, but at least we can play with them when we're together."

Dad's email message congratulated Hugh and Margie Quenton on the new assignment and said he looked forward to seeing them and Suzie Q again. He thanked them again for their condolences after Chad and Kate's mom's death eight months earlier, then added, "While it won't be the same without her when we get together, we'll have lots of fond memories to share. Don't hesitate to talk about her, as so many people around here do. I suppose they think it's too painful for me, but the truth is, there's nothing I'd rather do than think and talk about Kathryn."

Chad scrolled down to read the rest of Dad's message.

"We'll give you time to settle in and get your bearings, and then we'll try to drive over there the weekend after next. We'll leave Friday after school and probably see you late that night."

AirQuest Adventures

Travel 'round the world with twelve-year-old Chad, his younger sister, Kate, and their risk-taking, entrepreneur dad as the three go globe-trotting to help those in need—and land in more trouble than they ever imagined!

Crash at Cannibal Valley

ISBN 0-310-71347-1

In the first book of the AirQuest Adventures, after their plane goes down in Indonesia, Chad must help his injured sister and his dad survive in an area rumored to be inhabited by cannibals.

Disaster at the Yukon

ISBN 0-310-71345-5

In the third book of the AirQuest Adventures, when a blizzard cuts off communication and supplies, Chad and Dad are forced to make a perilous journey across land and sky to save a gravely ill friend.

Available at your local bookstore!
zonderkidz

zonder**kidz**®

We want to hear from you. Please send your comments
about this book to us in care of zreview@zondervan.com. Thank you.

Grand Rapids, MI 49530
www.zonderkidz.com

ZONDERVAN.COM/
AUTHOR**TRACKER**